THE GREEN
MEMORY OF FEAR

THE GREEN MEMORY OF FEAR

B.A. CHEPAITIS

WILDSIDE PRESS

THE GREEN MEMORY OF FEAR

To the survivors: Sisters, brothers, friends, self.

I release you, my beautiful and terrible fear. I release you. You were my beloved and hated twin, but now I don't know you as myself. I release you with all the pain I would know at the death of my daughters.

You are not my blood anymore.
I Give you Back, Joy Harjo, **She Had Some Horses**

PROLOGUE

Home Planet—Manhattan, USA

IT WAS A MUGGY DAY IN THE CITY, and all around the smell of urine, the smell of hot tar was in the air.

He paused in the street to stare up at a skyscraper, his eyes straining through the glare that bounced off the windows. This wasn't the building he wanted, but it was near here. He sensed it in his skin, the remnants of a memory still palpable to him.

The little girl at his side tugged at his sleeve. He looked down as if he'd forgotten her.

"I'm hungry," she said.

"Soon," he said. "We'll eat soon."

She scratched at her arm. She wouldn't whine. She never whined. She had other ways of showing her displeasure. He reached for her hand and she let him take it, but she dragged her feet as they walked. He made a sound of complaint, but he didn't slap her the way he usually would. That put her on alert, made her wonder what was wrong.

They crossed 73rd street, went down three blocks and turned right. When they reached the building he wanted he stood in front of it looking up, holding the little girl's hand. The people who passed by made no note of them. They were just two of the millions who lived or worked or walked in New Manhattan, just a small, rather mousy girl and a medium built, almost deliberately nondescript man in his early fifties. He ignored them too. He had other business to attend to. Someone he wanted to find. Someone who once lived here.

After all these years he could still catch the scent of her, so specific and so telling. The scent of an empath. A girl child with something wild in her soul.

He breathed it in deeply, and as he breathed, he remembered.

He'd seen her during the marvelous wreck of the Killing Times in Manhattan, when murder was the only means left to create human connection, the last ritual act in a world gone spiritually dead. In a final desperate attempt to feel alive the people killed and killed and killed again. It was a beautiful thing to behold, an ecstasy of blood and triumph, and there was nothing like it before or since.

While it went on he fed off it insatiably, growing ever more powerful. By the time he caught the scent of the empath girl he was as strong as he would ever be. Though their meeting was brief, his memory of it was precise and delicious to this day.

Many years had passed since then. She would be a grown woman now. He wondered if she remembered him at all. If not, he would remind her when they met again.

At his side, the little girl shifted from foot to foot impatiently.

He gave her arm a quick jerk. "Quiet, child," he said. "You need to know her, too. That's why I brought you here."

She wiggled, pulling her hand from his, but he grasped her wrist and held her.

"Look," he said, pointing up. "She lived there. Can you smell it?"

The girl turned her face up. "No," she said.

"Then be quiet and let me enjoy myself." He closed his eyes and breathed in.

She had been young and full of energy, her empathic gifts developed well beyond her years. She would be an implacable enemy, an invaluable ally, but that wasn't the only reason he sought her. In all the time since then, she was the one scent he couldn't define and had never found again.

"I don't smell anything except dog crap," the little girl said.

He ignored her, though he knew she was right. Here, where they stood, was nothing but his memory and crap. She'd been carried away in fire and the storm of time. He wouldn't find her here, and the girl at his side would learn nothing more from viewing the past. They should move on.

"Come, child." He turned away from the building and walked down the street.

"Are we gonna get some food?" she asked. "There's hot dogs." She pointed at a vendor.

His face expressed distaste. "That's not how we feed."

She was the most capable of all his children, and the most stubborn. She wouldn't hunt. She refused to sex or be sexed. If he tried she clawed and bit and screeched abysmally. Threats of death were useless because she was entirely ready to die. But recently he'd found something more potent than death to sway her. He'd given her hope, in lethal doses, and that would ultimately make her do as he wished.

"If you want to see her, you'll learn to feed as I say," he told her.

"I want a hot dog," she insisted.

"What do you want more—a hot dog, or a mother?" he asked.

She was sullen, silent. That, she understood.

"If it's a mother, pay attention," he said. "I'll show you how it's done."

The city, so full of energy, was the best place to feed and to sex. For today, however, he'd just feed. Though sexing was infinitely more enjoyable and the best source of food, immediately after it left him languid, indolent with pleasure, and he wanted to stay alert.

As he walked with the girl he sniffed for food, and soon enough he bumped into a well-heeled, well-suited woman passing by. He grasped her arm and smiled at her. "Sorry," he said.

Her face went white and her breathing briefly ceased. He released her and she stood swaying, then righted herself.

"Quite alright," she replied, and walked on.

He sighed. A small feed, but it worked.

The little girl wrinkled her nose at him. "I want a hot dog," she insisted. "With ketchup."

He put a hand to her head as if to pat it, then quickly grabbed her hair and jerked her back. When he released her she fell forward onto her knees. He bent down to her. An older woman with white hair and a kind smile stopped near them.

"Do you need help?" she asked.

He lifted his face and smiled. "She tripped," he said.

The woman instinctively reached out to the child. He put the girl's hand on the woman's arm, with his over it. She would feel the feeding whether she wanted to or not. This kind of energy was best for the kind of work he wanted from her. At his touch, the woman swayed, her pupils dilating. After a few seconds he released her. That would be enough.

"Thank you," he said to the woman. "I appreciate it."

"No problem," she said, looking a little dazed as she walked away.

He turned back to the girl. Her face was mottled white and red. "I'm gonna be sick," she said.

"No," he commanded, but it did no good.

She gulped twice, then leaned over and retched on the sidewalk at his feet. People walking by looked at them, then away.

"You're disgusting," he whispered while he held her hair back and pretended to be solicitous. "How will you find a mother if you can't do the simplest thing I ask?"

She sobbed, and he stepped away, waiting impatiently while her crying slowed and finally subsided. Then he grabbed her neck and squeezed. "Are you done, idiot?" he whispered.

She nodded. He released her and they walked on. She was irritating, insolent, difficult, but she wasn't entirely without sense. She'd cooperate in the end.

Tomorrow they'd return to his house in Toronto. Tonight, while they were still in Manhattan, he'd show her how to bring him what he wanted, see if she could get the job done. But for now he'd remember the days when the streets swelled with the stench of death, when so many of those bound to him ruled the city and stealing green from the bodies of children was as simple as a smile.

And even if the girl would not feed, he would.

He walked until he found an alley littered with garbage and stench. Here, they squatted down against a wall and waited for darkness, and his dinner.

Planetoid Three—Toronto Replica, Zone 12

Jaguar Addams walked in slow circles around her prisoner. He sat on the floor in the center of her circle, eyes glazed, mouth hanging open.

"This is the easy part," she crooned, the gold flecks in her green eyes glittering in the candlelight. "We're just on the surface now."

He moaned softly.

"Hurt?" she asked.

His head moved up and down in something resembling a nod.

"Good," she said, and extended her hand, two fingers moving toward his forehead.

She'd been working with this prisoner for four weeks and finally thought she could see an end in sight. He was a pedophile who strangled a girl while raping her. His wife found the little girl's underwear in his jacket pocket and called the police. It was a straightforward case that even the Planetoid Prison testers named correctly. He feared death, and clung to children as sexual partners in order to live within the illusion of perpetual youth. That was common in pedophiles. That, and fear of powerlessness were the two fears she most frequently had to make them meet in this prison system where criminals were rehabbed by facing their fears.

And she knew how to bring them there.

She was the one Teacher on Prison Planetoid 3 who had a consistent success rate with pedophiles. Either repugnance or lack of skill kept most Teachers from getting the job done, while Jaguar used her highly developed talents in the empathic arts to bring these men to the deepest part of their shadowed selves. Alex, her supervisor and a good enough empath that he ought to know better, was always nagging her about the danger of getting shadow sickness from such contact, but Jaguar found she'd get nowhere without it. Other techniques were totally ineffective. Even the newer meds shifted only their chemistry, but not their souls.

Jaguar wanted to shift their souls. She intoned the ritual words that would begin to do so with this prisoner.

"See who you are," she said, "Be what you see."

She reached for him, her sea-green eyes holding him still. The air in the room grew thick with the low hum of human energy in motion.

Then, a voice called her name.

From somewhere clear as a night emptied of stars, a child's voice called her.

Jaguar.

She went still, her focus dissipated.

Jaguar. We need you.

"Who is it?" she whispered.

Hurry Jaguar. We're waiting for you.

"Where?" she sent back.

No answer. Laughter ran through her. Near the bookshelves that lined her living room wall she saw motion, small and quick, like a darting hummingbird. A book shook itself loose and fell to the floor. Her eyes were sharp enough to read the title on the spine.

The Etiquette of Vampires, by Lale Davidson.

Her prisoner blinked, saw his opportunity and lunged for her. And for the next few minutes she was too busy with her job to think of anything else.

CHAPTER 1

"TAKING UP A NEW HOBBY?" ALEX ASKED, picking up a book from the coffee table in Jaguar's living room.

On top of the book, *The Etiquette of Vampires*, was a disc titled *Vampires of the World*.

Jaguar, who was bringing a tray with honey and cups of tea from the kitchen to the living room, stopped and scanned all six feet and one inch of him, from his thick dark hair to his good black shoes. Then she brought her glance up to stay with his angular face and coal dark eyes. Alex, accustomed to her occasional need to visually frisk him for weapons, waited it out.

"Know anything about vampires?" she asked.

"That depends," he said.

"On what?"

"On what kind you mean. The Draculas, the Japanese river creatures, the lamia. Or maybe you mean the twenty-first century romantic version?"

"Not those," she said, and she moved toward the coffee table with her burden. "There's no glitter in the beast, if you ask me."

"Okay, then. Maybe the Windigo—or the Greenkeepers, as they're called."

Jaguar set the tray down on the coffee table and curled herself into a chair, inviting Alex to take the couch. "Apparently you do know something about them," she said as he sat.

He tossed the book on the table between them. "I like to read, too. Did you get through Davidson yet?"

"Some of it. I had a prisoner to deal with."

"So why are you interested in vampires?" he asked.

She poured honey into her spoon and stirred her tea with it. "Idle curiosity," she said, and he laughed.

"What's wrong with that?" she demanded, viewing him over her spoon as she licked the remaining honey off it.

"Nothing, except I don't believe you. You never do anything idly. You're very goal-oriented. Which kind of vampires are you interested in?"

"And you're as persistent as a truffle hunting pig. What difference does it make which vampire?"

"It'll tell me what I have to worry about. For instance, if you're researching Windigo, a Native species, it's probably for ritual purposes and my level of concern remains low."

"Windigo aren't Mertec. My people had a different name for it."

"I'm aware of that. But Davidson doesn't have a section on the earth-eater. In fact, I might be the only white man in the world who knows about it."

She reached across the table and traced a star on his forehead. "Consider it a gold one," she said. "And if I'm interested in Lamias?"

"You're not, are you?" he asked.

She retreated into herself, stirring her tea. He reached across the table and touched her wrist as he let his thoughts slip into hers.

What is it? he asked, subvocally.

He felt her sharp retraction, and quickly, courteously, he bowed out. But not before he retrieved a piece of information he'd been seeking.

He leaned back in his chair, picked up his tea. "Why are you interested in Greenkeepers?"

"The Adept at work," she muttered.

She considered his precognitive capacities the most manipulative of the empathic arts and continued to distrust them, with feeling.

"I don't think I'm the only one working, chant-shaper," he answered.

She kept her gaze away from his. He tapped his spoon against the table. She raised her head and lifted a corner of her mouth in a smile. Deliberately neutral, except for her eyes, which studied him hard.

He knew that look. She was waiting to see his next move before she made any of her own. Her ego allowed her to make very few false moves. And right now, it was entirely possible that she was afraid of him, for the same reasons he was afraid of her.

No. Not afraid of her. Afraid of what he felt about her.

They'd worked together for over six years, been very good friends for at least five, and slept together once. Just once. Enough to tell them both that kind of interaction wasn't something to take or leave lightly.

A few months had passed since then, and the only agreement they'd reached was to go neither forward nor backwards. She'd been aloof, and he'd been polite and distant. They were engaged in a complex dance on a trembling plane, waiting to see if the earth would stop its tectonic motion any time soon, or if they could find new footing on it.

For his part, he'd also been watching for her fur to settle after the intensity of their last encounter, which had served to save both their lives. He approached her as he would any wild thing, with slow and deliberate care. She needed time to know she could negotiate the turf of what would be a totally new geography of the emotions for them both. And right now, she needed to know what he knew about Greenkeepers.

She stretched her legs out, the material of her long, loose dress rippling like water over them. Her gaze was open and clear as ocean, and just as impossible to fathom. Her silence was extravagant and complete. She was waiting for him to come up with something. He obliged.

"The Greenkeeper," he said, "is a deceptively gentle name for modern North American vampires. They were first written about after the Serials, when quite a few of the earliest murderers brought in claimed they used ritual rape and murder to regenerate themselves physically. Nothing proven, of course, but theoretically Greenkeepers can use energy transfer, blood, or sexual fluids to trigger cellular regeneration. They prefer children, because they've got more of the right stuff than adults. The name," he concluded, "is from the response of regenerative biochemicals to lab experiments."

He took her hand and lifted his teacup over it, pouring a stream of green tea to pool in her palm. "When isolated, they turn green."

She stared at her palm, then tipped it to let the tea flow into the saucer under his cup. She closed her eyes and pressed the index finger of her right hand against her lips, tapped them as if sounding morse code. Alex waited. When she reopened her eyes, they were still neutral.

"Pedophiles were some of the earliest ritual killers during the Serials. So how do you tell the difference between a pedophile and a Greenkeeper?" she asked.

"Is that a riddle?"

"No. I'm asking. How?"

That was an unexpected question. He searched his rather extensive memory to see what emerged. Jonathan Post, in his book *Unparticular Magic*, said early 21st literature that romanticized vampires reflected the larger cultural attraction to pedophilia. Other historians noted that rates for child abuse were higher previous to the Killing Times than at any other time in history. They calculated how many of those abused went on to become abuser, who were released from overcrowded prisons just before the violence erupted.

But pedophiles were a dime a dozen, while even Davidson admitted that Greenkeepers were rare, if they existed at all. They either had to be born with the inherent capacity to access regenerative material, or transformed into that skill by another Greenkeeper. And unlike any other psi capacity, they never turned out well.

They were an anomaly, born to evil in a universe that preferred the good. And their relationship to pedophiles was, theoretically at least, complex.

"While all Greenkeepers are pedophiles," he said, "Not all pedophiles are Greenkeepers. Greenkeepers have lots of psi capacities—Telekinesis, shapeshifting, hypnopathy, Protean change—and pedophiles don't. Of course, one Greenkeeper can do damage on a scale beyond the pedophile's wildest dream, because theoretically they live as long as they keep feeding. And they rarely transform those they feed from. They just bind them at an energy level so they'll go on to become destructive, but without the powers of their master. That means pedophiles could be former victims of Greenkeepers, bound but not transformed."

"What happened to the ones brought in during the Killing Times?" she asked.

"You mean the ones who claimed they were Greenkeepers?" he amended.

"Yes," she agreed. "Those, if you insist on reasonable doubt."

Alex held his hands palm up. "They disappeared."

She nodded, as if she expected this answer.

"That doesn't mean anything," he said. "You disappeared, too. More than ten million people disappeared, one way and another. Everything was in chaos."

The Killing Times they'd both survived—she as a teenager, he as a young man—left the major cities of North America in upheaval for years. The rise in serial killing from which it derived its name was followed by uncontainable violence, domestic terrorism, burning and death. Keeping track of mythical Greenkeepers was the last thing on anyone's mind.

"Besides," he added, "even Davidson admits there's no actual proof of their existence. All the evidence is anecdotal. Like ghost stories and UFOs."

"Sexual abuse stats plunged like a rock after the Killing Times," she said, "and now they're climbing again, along with incidence of violent crime in children."

As usual, she knew her facts. In the last year New York state alone put ten children on trial for murder. He'd sat on two committee meetings to discuss whether juvies should go to the Planetoids. Jaguar said they should send the parents up instead.

"Are you suggesting a Greenkeeper's responsible for that?" he asked.

"I'm speculating about possibilities, great and small. Does Davidson offer any ideas for capture or cure?"

"No cure. There is none. And capture is difficult. Theoretically they can regenerate wounds rapidly, so bullets won't work. If you keep one locked up long enough without feeding maybe they'll dissipate for lack of energy—a kind of starvation—but try keeping them locked up if they really can shapeshift. Stories say salt burns them—a bad interaction with their biochem—but it won't kill them. Also they fear snakes because systemic poisoning makes quick regeneration difficult. But according to Davidson the only viable way to deal with them is your ancestor's treatment."

"Which one?"

"Rip their hearts out," he said. "Basically you have to do enough damage rapidly enough that they can't regenerate. Getting as close as you need to do that without being killed is the tough part. You only get one shot at a Greenkeeper."

"Right," she said. Then, "How do you happen to have all this information at your fingertips?" she asked. "Idle curiosity?"

He was going to try that answer, but since she'd anticipated it, he went for the truth instead. "About a week ago I picked up Davidson and read it through," he answered. "I don't know what impelled me, but it did seem important at the time."

She raised an eyebrow at him. He understood the question in her face, which asked whether this was from Adept space, a precognitive sense that this knowledge would be needed soon. In the absence of a definite answer he merely shrugged.

She accepted that in silence. She stood and walked over to the window, where she stared out over the replica city of Toronto, built to mimic the original for this zone of Planetoid 3. The sun was dipping over the horizon, the buildings washed in soft gold.

"I still want to know why *you're* interested," he noted. "If you think your current prisoner shows tendencies that way, that'd be important."

"No. Nothing like that. Just—the book fell off the shelf."

He supposed that wouldn't mean anything to anyone else, but he understood. Empaths were trained to pay attention to small signals. When books leapt off shelves at your feet, you picked them up and read them, even if there didn't seem any reason to do so. Later, you might find out that part of the shelf wasn't level. Or you might find this was exactly the information you needed. Either way, knowing the reason behind her curiosity settled his nerves, for now. It could also explain his sudden interest in reading the same book. Their history together included a great deal of close empathic contact, and that sometimes created interesting synchronicities.

"Did you like the Davidson book?" she asked after a while.

"Very much. It's an evil kind of creature, but her writing's always beautiful, so it's worth the read. I think," he noted more philosophically, "beauty may be the only antidote there is to evil."

"That's a romantic notion," she said.

"Then I'm a romantic. But you knew that, didn't you?"

His tone gave him away. She turned to him, her face full of questions. She started with the most obvious one. "You didn't come over to talk about vampires, did you?"

He leaned back and asked his breathing to normalize itself, asked his heart rate to slow down. After all their circling dance, today he was ready to call some new steps. It wasn't as easy as he thought it would be.

They shared friends and work and knowledge in the empathic arts. They shared assignments and risks and rescues. One way and another, they spent more time together than apart. Their high regard for each other had even survived sleeping together. And here he was, skittish as spit on a griddle about asking her out.

"No. I wanted to see if you'd like to have dinner with me," he said.

She tried to absorb the question and failed. It was already past dinnertime. "Dinner?" she repeated.

"Later this week. I was thinking *La Loba*. You said you like their Tequila."

He saw complexities cross her thoughts as she chewed the inside of her lip. She wasn't getting it.

"I'm asking you out, Jaguar," he said, his voice like gravel in his throat. "On a date."

"Oh," she said. "Oh."

And then, silence, as she stared at her hands.

At least, he thought, he had the satisfaction of seeing her shocked into speechlessness. That was a rare and precious moment. He savored it briefly, then asked, "Is Thursday good? "

She conducted another interview with her emotions, and although they weren't in empathic contact, he could guess the nature of her thoughts. They probably weren't much different than his, which asked him repeatedly what confused sense of chivalry impelled him to do this.

He had other options. She'd be amenable to something casual, to being intermittent lovers with no strings attached. They'd stay friends and nothing much would change. And she wouldn't push if he let it drop altogether. Eventually it would disappear, swallowed by his favorite ally, time. But to try and establish something real between them could be pure and gallant stupidity of the most egregious kind. To say I want this, and I want it real was probably the last thing she expected, and the most foolhardy thing he could do.

He waited, while her internal conversation rounded itself out to resolution.

"I'm singing with *Moon Illusion* on Thursday," she said at last. She regularly sang with this band of former prisoners so it was a valid excuse, but his disappointment was sharp. He was debating what to say next when she breached the gulf of silence.

"How's Wednesday?" she asked.

He let his pulse steady itself, then raised himself from his chair to leave.

"Wednesday's good," he said. "See you about seven, if that's okay."

"Sure," she said. "Seven's fine. See you then."

He thought about saying more, but she'd already turned away. Enough, he thought. Enough for now.

He moved toward the door, and let himself out.

CHAPTER 2

THE PLANETOID ATMOSPHERE, CREATED THROUGH a mass generator, had spit out a hot day. On Wednesday morning Jaguar stood in heavy humidity on Yonge street, staring at a bronze and gold silk pantsuit in a store window as the sun pressed against the back of her neck.

She'd woken early to finish her final report on her last assignment, then decided to take care of a few errands downtown. She was almost done when she was captured by the outfit in the window of *Wild Child Boutique*.

She pressed a hand against the glass. Shimmering bronze and gold washed silk, pants and sleeveless top, perfectly cut. Simple as air.

"That would look so good on me," she murmured. The color worked for her eyes and complexion, the silk was good for her skin, and the cut was right for her lean and muscular body. It looked comfortable, too. Easy to wear, without too many moving parts.

She went into the store, found her size, and tried it on. When she emerged, she was bearing a package and smiling. A good day. Her work was done, and the outfit was hers.

A steamy breeze ruffled the hair at the back of her neck in a friendly way. She tilted her head back and took in a good breath. She'd spent her adolescence in New Mexico, her childhood in Manhattan. She knew the heat of the mesas, the crowded streets, and the sweat lodge, and she liked them all. Today's heat in particular seemed to hold a promise she wanted to take in, though she couldn't name it. Whatever it was, it made her steps light and easy.

She went through her mental lists of other tasks to perform. License renewal, a physical training session. Maybe tonight she'd have dinner with her friend Rachel.

But no. There was something else she was supposed to do tonight. She frowned, trying to recapture elusive memory. Something important, she thought. Something she had a nagging feeling she was nervous about, which might be why she was inclined to forget it. The air tickled her neck, and the sun patted warmly at her back. It would come to her. If not, she'd look it up on her calendar when she got home. She hoped she remembered to put it in. She walked on.

As she neared the Teacher's building where she'd go for training she felt a drop in heat. She glanced up and saw dark clouds clustering over the high buildings. She stopped at a corner and peered up at them. If it was a storm, it was moving fast. Like great shadows of wings flying low over the buildings.

She glanced at the people walking past her. They smiled and nodded, no disturbance in their faces. She turned back to the darkening sky and felt an encroaching cold wrap her skin. Not a cloud. Something living. Something unpleasant. She wanted to run, get under cover fast because this felt like terror about to swallow her whole. Then, a voice, stopping her.

Jaguar. Here.

That voice. She'd heard it in her apartment not too long ago. The voice of a little girl.

Jaguar.

She held herself still against her own fear. "Who is it?" she asked.

It's me, Jaguar. Here. Look.

She scanned the street to her left, her right, behind her. Traffic moved along the road and overhead. People passed, heels clicking against cement. They noticed nothing wrong. Whatever was going on was just for her.

Right in front of you. It's me.

There. Dead ahead, standing in the middle of the sidewalk facing her.

A little girl, maybe eleven years old, wearing a grey and red checked dress. No shoes. Long mousy hair partially obscuring a very pale heart-shaped face, with large dark eyes, eyes full of shadows. Behind her, darkness shimmered, as if she'd emerged from it.

There weren't many children here. The facilities for accommodating them were limited, so seeing a child alone on the streets was unusual. Even more unusual was her dress.

"That's my dress," Jaguar murmured. "I had that dress."

She remembered the pattern and texture. It was her favorite. She was wearing it when she ran out of her apartment in Manhattan, leaving her grandparent's dead bodies behind.

"Why are you wearing my dress?" she called and the girl turned and scampered away.

Jaguar trotted after her, reaching out subvocally. *Wait. Tell me what you want. Don't run away.*

Again that laughter, watery and bright. Jaguar kept moving, pushing people out of her way as she went. The girl turned a corner and Jaguar followed until she found herself in a long alley. The girl stood at the far end. She lifted her hand and pointed down.

Look, Jaguar. For you.

Jaguar looked down. A newspaper had wrapped itself around her ankle. She reached for it and saw a headline.

PSYCHIATRIST TO STAND TRIAL.

Under the headline was a picture of a man who was perhaps fifty, more or less. He held a hand out in a gesture of negation. Warding off journalists, Jaguar thought. His name was Dr. Thomas Senci.

She grabbed the paper and held it up to ask the little girl about it, but she was gone. And when Jaguar looked down at her hand, so was the newspaper.

She rubbed her fingers together. They could still feel the paper between them. She looked down the alley. Nobody was there. She was alone. She scanned the sky. The darkness was gone, too. She walked back onto the street.

Somebody, she thought, wanted to tell her something. "Okay," she murmured. "I'll bite."

It was easy enough for her to find out about Dr. Senci. If he was standing trial for anything serious he'd already be in the Planetoid files. They tracked all cases that might end up here.

She stopped and hailed a cab, which took her to the Planetoid offices. Once inside, she made her way to the computer research room in the basement, found a screen and punched in her code.

"May I be of assistance?" the computer asked.

"No vocalization, please," Jaguar said before she could stop herself. Alex always said please to the computers and apparently she'd caught the habit, though she'd told him the computer didn't give a rat's ass. He did, he said. It reminded him of the importance of courtesy.

"Voicebox shutdown," the computer said, and was silent.

Jaguar went to the prelim area and keyed in the name Senci. The same picture she'd seen in the newspaper appeared on screen, along with information on his case. The charges—child molestation—made it clear why he was in their files already. All pedophiles were shunted to the Planetoid system these days, and most of them to Planetoid 3. What they did was much more effective than anything the home planet could offer, and the home planet was glad enough to get rid of them.

Dr. Thomas Senci, a neuropsychologist, was being charged with sexual abuse of a twelve year old boy who was his patient. That charge was seen as more pertinent in Planetoid terms because Senci had also recently been investigated for murder conspiracy because four of his other patients, all boys between the ages of 12 and 16, had gone on a killing spree, spreading laser fire around a fast-food restaurant. When the body count was totaled fourteen people were dead, including the boys, who had killed themselves.

One remaining patient—a boy of 13—said Dr. Senci asked him to participate in the killing but he refused. That boy's diagnosis of paranoid schizophrenia ended up discrediting his claim, so the charges against

Senci weren't pursued, but they made the Provincial prosecuting attorney more amenable to trying the new charge of sexual abuse. The identity of the boy charging him was being shielded from the public. Further reading told her Senci's information had already gone to the testers, which meant odds were high for a conviction.

Jaguar contemplated the face on the computer screen and asked the imaging program to turn it half right. This gave her a projected image of his full face. She considered it, and requested hard copy of that, and his folder. Medical records, fingerprints, employment history, one more photo, rolled out of the printer. There was as yet no psychological profile.

Staring at his photo gave her a slight queasiness, and a feeling of something familiar. Had she seen him somewhere? She was generally good at remembering faces, but she couldn't place this one. She put it away and went back to the computer screen. If she chased it, it would elude her. Whatever it was would be visible in time.

The end of the report gave a place where Planetoid researchers could sign up if they were interested in conducting the preliminary research. Whoever got the job would do interviews, create a personality profile and a narrative account of the trial, slated for two weeks hence, for use here if he was convicted.

Her hand paused. She didn't do research. She was a Teacher, not a note taker. So she always said. Somewhere in the empty room, she heard a scuttling sound.

Are you ready, Jaguar?

The queasiness grew stronger. Her hands moved on the keys, typing her name in.

"Ready when you are," she answered.

* * * *

The next person to visit the computers was team member Rachel Shofet, who was updating preliminary files for her zone.

Rachel always claimed she hadn't a bit of empath in her. She was just lucky. In this case, she was utilizing the bank of computers only because her own was getting its annual servicing today. And though she had no idea she'd just missed Jaguar, didn't notice the keyboards were still warm from her fingers, couldn't pick up on what an empath would detect as the most obvious signs of her presence, she did notice the Senci case had an applicant for prelimary researcher.

"Jaguar?" she asked it. Something odd there. She'd been both a co-worker and friend to Jaguar for many years, and knew she never took research assignments.

Rachel tapped on the desk and thought. She usually sent files electronically to Alex's computer so he could look at them on his own schedule and dole out assignments accordingly. This one she printed out as hard copy, and walked it upstairs to his office.

She knocked on his door, heard his voice, and stepped inside.

"Hey," she said, "What's Jaguar got to do with Dr. Senci?"

Alex, head bent over his computer, regarded her vaguely. "Another riddle?" he asked.

"What?" Rachel said.

"Never mind. What about Jaguar?"

Rachel tossed the paper on his desk. "Look at that," she said.

He scanned it, saw Jaguar's name. He also knew she avoided research like the plague, unless it was unofficial research into a topic that tickled her personal fancy. Like the rings of Saturn. Or varieties of mint. Or Greenkeepers.

"What's he being tried for?" Alex asked.

"Child molestation. Your basic pedophile, it looks like. The Medical Board acts as judiciary panel, but it's a criminal trial. Toronto's system is strange."

"Strange," Alex agreed. He thought about riddles, like how do you tell the difference between a pedophile and a Greenkeeper.

"What do you think?" Rachel asked. "Why'd she sign up for it?"

"I don't know," he said. "I'll ask her tonight."

"Tonight?"

"We're going out."

"Out?"

"To dinner. I'll ask her. I think." He paused. Was it protocol to ask why she was lying about her interest in vampires while they were on their first date? He rubbed his hand over his face.

"Going out?" Rachel repeated.

He raised an eyebrow at her, dared her to comment.

Rachel tucked her lower lip under her teeth, then released it. "Oh," she said. "Then, I can probably have it for you in an hour or so."

"Did I ask for something, Rachel?"

"No," she said. "But I figured you'd want the full file on Senci. And I'd suggest that blue shirt with the salamander design on the sleeve. It's a great color for your eyes."

She turned and left, while Alex took a moment to thank all available deities that Rachel wasn't an empath. She was dangerous enough as it was.

CHAPTER 3

By THE TIME JAGUAR LEFT the Planetoid office and got back to her apartment, she felt as if someone had pulled the plug on her energy core. The queasiness was passing, but her fatigue was inexplicable, and the joints in her wrist hurt, as if leaching out poisons. She wondered if she was still getting rid of the toxic waste from her last prisoner, a difficult case. She went to her kitchen and made tea from a blend of cleansing herbs One Bird taught her.

She drank the mix, a bitter tasting remedy, then went directly to her bedroom, stripped off her clothes and wrapped herself in a gold silk bathrobe before she fell onto the bed. She dropped into sleep like a stone, only to be woken repeatedly by a series of disconnected dreams, all of them ugly. They woke her, then woke her again until she stuffed her face into her pillow and groaned, "Christ, just let me sleep, will you?"

She gave it up when a dream of being telecommed by a horse in judge's robes morphed into her own telecom buzzing, waking her for good. She twisted to her clock. 6 pm. Shit. She hadn't been in bed that long, had she? She sat up and held her head. At least she felt better. Not nauseated. Not exhausted.

"Okay," she said. "I'm awake." She sat up, made sure her robe covered what she wanted covered, went to the telecom and pressed the receive button. Alex's face appeared on screen.

He scanned her. "Good nap?" he asked.

She ruffled her hair further. "More like adventures in dreamland. What's up?"

"We are," he said, "or did you forget?"

She scanned the back of her eyelids for information. What she was booked for. Dinner with Alex. A date.

"You forgot, didn't you Jaguar?"

"No," she said. "I just didn't believe you."

"You thought I was kidding?"

"Maybe."

"Maybe not. Serious as the plague."

"Alex, are you sure this is a good idea?"

"No," he said. "Not at all. I'll pick you up in an hour."

"We're taking your wings?" she asked.

"Yes," he said, trying to leave no room for discussion.

"I don't like wings," she noted.

He moved his lips away from his teeth in a close approximation of a tolerant smile. "Would you prefer to take your car and meet me at the restaurant?"

"Yes," she said. "I would."

"Right. Then let's. It's La Loba. In case you forgot. In an hour."

"Okay. I might be a little late. I have to get dressed."

He looked at the gold bathrobe she was clutching to herself. "That color's nice on you," he suggested.

She looked down at the robe, then narrowed mischievous eyes at him. "You'll be sorry for that," she said, and clicked off.

* * * *

When she made her way across the restaurant to where Alex sat, he almost forgot to breathe. She wore silk the way some women wear skin, and the gold of her pantsuit was not far removed in tone or in proximity from her skin. It deepened the green of her eyes, caught at the gold in her hair, which caught at the air in his throat. He rose from his chair and gave her the bow she deserved.

She lifted her gaze and he felt the brush of her thoughts against his. Just fishing. Just seeing what was hanging around. Her mouth twitched into a smile.

"I would've worn the robe," she said, "but it was wrinkled because I slept in it. I haven't slept in this. Yet."

"Yet," he repeated hopefully, and then walked over to pull her chair out for her, letting his hand rest briefly on her shoulder after she was seated. She didn't shove him away in response, so he advanced to a caress.

She opened her menu and said, without raising her head, "If you air kiss me, I'll kill you."

"When I kiss you there won't be any air involved," he replied as he returned to his chair.

So far, he thought, so good. She would keep it light. Stick to the surface like an Olympic skater. Probably he'd enjoy it immensely. By the time the waiter came by and they ordered their tequila and dinner, he knew he was right. She got the lobster. He'd seen her eat lobster before. Predation and sensuality, both at their best.

"So what do we talk about?" she asked after the first shot of tequila was down, "First date, right? Politics are a no-no. Religion's touchy."

"Maybe we should try sports," Alex suggested.

"No good. You're a Packer Backer. I favor the Jaguars. You'll just get pissed off when I talk about winning."

"Packers have more experience. More staying power. You know that."

"And once Jaguar's latch on, they don't let go. Not until they're dead."

"I'm not especially worried about that," he said.

Arrival of their dinners interrupted further debate and, eschewing the bib, she cracked a claw and pulled white meat from the shards with her fingers. She dipped it in butter and licked the meat, the ends of her fingers, her own lips. Alex felt deep contentment.

"If sports are out, then what do you suggest?" she asked.

"We can start with the courtesies. That outfit looks lovely on you."

"Thank you," she said, and ripped a leg off the lobster, sucked meat from the end of it.

He leaned an elbow on the table and rested his chin on his hand. "You like lobster, don't you?"

She cracked the tail and used her fingers to pull out thick pieces of sweet flesh. "One man said it made him sick to his stomach to watch me eat it."

"Some men," Alex suggested, "have weak stomachs. Me—I'm just enjoying the show."

She continued to pursue her pleasure. Talk turned to food and its preparation, meandered from there to good wine, strolled toward music and always stayed on the safest grounds. Alex didn't mind, as long as the lobster held out. When it was gone, he sighed, but regained his interest when the waiter brought chocolate mousse, which she savored in small lipfuls sucked from the end of her finger.

"Good?" he asked her.

"Very," she replied. "But you haven't eaten much. Not to your liking?"

He shook his head. "I'm distracted."

"By?"

He gestured toward the mousse. "The show," he said. Then, to his own dismay, he kept talking. "That, and something at work."

Jaguar's finger paused in its journey toward her mouth. "Oh?" she asked.

He knew what he was about to say, knew he shouldn't say it, and said it anyway. "One of my teacher's done something out of character," he said. "Way out. I want to know why."

He listened to himself talk with some amazement. He'd made up his mind not to bring up Dr. Senci. Apparently some part of him had vetoed his mind. He sincerely hoped it wasn't the Adept part. That wouldn't bode well.

"Who?" she asked.

"My best Teacher. She stays in the field. Never does research."

"I like her already."

"I thought you might. But she requested a research assignment today, gathering preliminary data on an accused pedophile. A Dr. Thomas Senci."

She finished licking her finger and stared at him. He didn't blame her. If he had a mirror, he'd stare at himself.

"News," she said, "travels too damn fast. I just punched it in this morning."

"Jaguar, I'm your supervisor. The request came to my office."

"Oh. Right."

"So tell me what it's all about."

She smoothed her hair back from her face and looked at him, then past him. They were co-workers again, suddenly and without much elbow-room.

"It's about a four week gig, Alex. I thought the change would be good for me. Keep me from going stale."

He tapped a finger against the table. "And what if I say no?"

She gazed down at his hand, pressed a finger against it. "Will you?" she asked.

He laid his hand, tense and flat, against the wood of the table. She continued to press her finger against it. She was so much better at putting up 'No Trespassing' signs than she was at reading them.

"I need to know why you want it before I decide," he said. "And you don't take research for fun, Jaguar, so try something else."

"You seem to know a lot about me, for a first date."

"I've had a few years of my own preliminary research. Look, if you want, we can talk about it tomorrow, in my office."

She sighed and stood up. "Get the bill, and meet me back at my place. I'll show you."

* * * *

Alex spent the ride to her apartment in a staff meeting with himself, asking questions about his general sanity. Like most staff meetings, everyone had a lot to say, and none of it was helpful. He ascended the stairs to her apartment and walked in the door, which was open for him.

"I'll make tea if you want some," she said when he was in.

"No thanks," he said, moving to a chair at her kitchen table. "I'll just sit and stew in my own juices."

"Suit yourself," she said, and crossed the living room to her desk. She opened a drawer and pulled out the Senci file, brought it to Alex. As she handed it over, he saw a tremor pass through her hand, up her arm. He opened the file and read. She stood at his back and waited motionless for his response.

He took his time, checking to make sure she hadn't gathered any information he didn't already have. When he was done, he closed the file and let his hands rest on it. Rachel had given him a more complete file, so for once he knew more than she did, except on one count—why she was interested. He decided to push at her about that.

"Not much of a case," he said. "A doctor who continues a successful practice in Toronto. Works with pre-teens to early adults, mostly on sequential dream modification and anxiety reduction programs."

"Yeah. He likes his clients young and scared. He moved to Toronto right after the Killing Times," she said. "He was at Columbia until—well, until the safety squads blew it up. Then he packed it in for Canada. Oh, Canada."

Alex could feel her at his back, motionless as ambient light, but bristling with anger. Canada gave a general amnesty less than a year after the dust settled from the Serials. No one would be prosecuted for the crimes committed during that time. Jaguar found that appalling.

"Lots of people left Manhattan after the Killing Times. Lots of them went to Toronto. That doesn't mean he's either a murderer or a pedophile. Besides, he still maintains a residence in New York."

"I know. He's a respected neuropsych specialist, and blah blah rat fuck blah."

"Since you've made your mind up about the Doctor, what do you know about the boy?" he asked.

She walked around to the table and sat across from him. "Nothing, yet. I'm not cleared for the information until my supervisor approves the assignment."

"*If* he approves," Alex amended. Then, "The boy's name is Daro Karas. Must be quite a kid because he got a voxchip recording of Dr. Senci admitting what he did. He's twelve, likes baseball, and his family would greatly prefer if he kept the hell out of it."

"How do you—" Jaguar started.

"—It's that supervisor thing," he cut in. "I'm cleared for all information—except why you're doing this. That's not in the files, so you'll have to fill in the blanks."

She stayed cool, casual. "I work a lot with pedophiles. It'd do me good to track one from the prelims. That's reasonable, isn't it?"

"Yes," Alex said. "And I'm guessing it's also true, since in fact you're a lousy liar. But you're a master of evasion, and I smell one here. There's more, isn't there?"

She'd known him long enough that she didn't deny it. "It's—complicated," she said.

"Like I'm not used to that? If you want the gig, you'll have to tell me."

She pressed the tips of two fingers against her forehead. Gesture of the empath. She went subvocal.

I'm called to it, Alex.

Show me, he requested.

She obliged, and he saw her chasing something into an alley. A little girl. Spirit child, by the feel of it. She wasn't solid—just an image projected into space. The girl disappeared and there was a newspaper flapping at Jaguar's ankles, an article about Dr. Senci visible.

"Okay," he said out loud. "I see."

She was called to it, by a spirit child. Not the sort of thing she'd fake for any reason. But it was, as she said, complicated. Senci had no record of molesting girls, for one thing, so who was this girl child and what did she have to do with the case? And what was she? Ghost, traveling thought, projection?

"Do you know the girl?" he asked.

"No. But she—she wears my clothes. Clothes I wore when I was a girl," she said. "I'll ask One Bird and Jake about it. See what they have to say."

If she planned to talk to Jake and One Bird, this was serious. She lived with them after her grandparents were killed in Manhattan, made her way from the City to their New Mexico village, mostly on foot, to find them. They were her guardians, her elders, her guides. He'd met them once when Jaguar took him to their village and he thought as highly of them as she did. They kept it simple, like the point of an arrow aimed at a bull's eye.

"Does this have anything to do with your interest in Greenkeepers?" he asked.

She startled just enough to scrape her chair back. That answered his question.

"All right," he said. "Tell me *what* this has to do with your interest in Greenkeepers."

She crossed her arms and glared at him. "Adepts," she said, "are so manipulative."

"And chant-shapers," he replied, "are so elusive. Tell me, Jaguar."

"It might be related," she said. "And it might not. I don't know yet. The two things occurred at the same time, but I'm not convinced they're causally connected. If I find out they are, I'll tell you."

"Jaguar," he said, "look at me."

She brought her eyes to focus on his, and he felt the force of their pull. That unrelenting, tidal pull. He let himself wash into it, skimming the surface of her emotions. They were turbulent, but not hidden. She was telling him the whole truth, as she knew it. This was all he was going to get.

He pushed his chair back from the table and stood to leave. "Okay," he said. "I'll grant the assignment. You'll be there a few weeks, but you'll keep in touch with me while you're away."

"Why?" she asked suspiciously.

"For one thing, it's procedure to report to your Supervisor when you're on a prelim. For another, I'll miss you."

"In that order?" she asked, still making light of it. But he didn't want to. Not anymore.

"There isn't any order for us, Jaguar. Just complexity, and maybe emotional chaos."

She ducked her head down and raised it up again. Reading him, just at the surface. One helluva date, he thought. He might as well finish it right.

He moved to where she sat, leaned down and kissed her, cupping her face in his hand and drawing her to him. When he let go, she pressed forward to him. A slight gesture, but he noticed and it gave him joy.

He reached for her hand, brought it to his lips, and kissed the back of it. Her breathing was finely controlled and her hand deliberately relaxed. He turned it palm up and traced the lifeline. With some satisfaction, he saw her shiver lightly at his touch.

"You have two breakpoints here," he noted.

"I'm aware of that," she said, voice low and husky. "One is from the Killing Times."

"And the other?" He pressed a finger against it, feeling the tingle that spread across her palm as she tensed slightly.

"I live dangerously."

"You do, in some ways," Alex agreed. "In other ways, you take the safest route possible."

He loosened his hold to give her the chance to gracefully retreat. When she didn't, he lifted her hand to his mouth and kissed the broken places, as if that would knit up the dangers into a solid and dependable line. Then he released her, and her hand dropped to her lap.

"It's been a pleasure having dinner with you Dr. Addams," he said. "I'll look forward to the next time. Maybe we'll try Porter's, for ribs and ice cream."

He turned to go, but the sudden stab of empathic contact stopped him from moving forward.

Alex?

Yes, Jaguar?

Her words were hesitant. *What are you doing?*

His reply, certain now, beyond all doubt.

I'm courting you.

A slow moment while she digested this, as if she was just catching on. As if she finally understood he meant this.

Courting me?

That's right. Any objections?

A pause in her thoughts as she retreated into herself to consider. Then, her response.

Not yet. I'll keep you posted as we go along.

She broke contact and he shuddered, feeling her absence.

"Goodnight," she said out loud. "I'll call you after I've met with the boy."

As he walked down the steps and out onto the street, he had the distinct impression that she stood at her window and watched him go.

* * * *

Jaguar packed after Alex left, putting the Davidson book, the Senci file, and a bag of dried mint in her bag along with her most formal business outfits, generally reserved for meetings with governors. She didn't like them. Didn't feel comfortable or able to move the way she wanted to when she wore office clothes. That, if nothing else, kept her away from research assignments. But she'd take this one, because a little girl led her to it. A girl with wild eyes, and a silver laugh.

"Wild child," she sang softly, "Full of grace. Savior of the human race."

Odd, that she should feel like singing. She liked the original version of Toronto much less than the Planetoid replica. The original was too polite and reserved, too much like a business suit for her to feel comfortable there. Here there were eccentrics, runaways, oddballs and people with wounds they'd honored and healed.

Occasionally she and Alex would go to the Planetoid eco-site, where the technicians kept the shield down and they could stare at the earth, that beautiful blue planet, spinning in space. It eclipsed all other stars, but Alex said that the people on earth viewed the Planetoid as a star, their population all star children.

Jaguar laughed, but she knew what he meant. Star children. Refugees from the blue planet. She supposed if she survived long enough, someday she'd get too old for her job and retire to New Mexico, stay in the village Jake and One Bird had established. Toronto, on the other hand, she could do without. Yet she'd chosen it. Because of a little girl with wild eyes who wore her dress, whose presence brought a dark and bitter wind.

And she felt like singing, in spite of that. Some emotion she couldn't name was surging to the surface, and it didn't feel quite in her control.

"It's idle curiosity," she said out loud. "That's all. I've never been courted before."

She continued to sing as she packed, and when she was done, she felt both tired and unable to sleep. She put her head down on the pillow anyway, hoping sleep would find her if she went through the motions.

Then weakness washed through her legs, and her stomach turned over.

"Hecate," she whispered. "What is it?"

She moved her glance around the room. There, at the foot of her bed. The little girl, this time wearing yellow pants and a red sleeveless top. Jaguar remembered them. They'd once been hers, too. But she looked different. Not playful at all. Her eyes were hungry and afraid.

We're waiting for you. Hurry.

Jaguar propped herself up on her elbows.

Wild child, she sang softly, *full of grace.*

The girl listened, then frowned.

Why are you singing that?

Because it's who you are.

The girl stared, her large dark eyes baskets of questions waiting to be filled with answers. And enough hunger to empty the whole world.

You are my wisdom, Jaguar said, not sure what she meant.

The girl lifted a hand, reaching out as if she could touch Jaguar, be touched by her.

I'm like you, she whispered. *We're the same.*

Jaguar nodded. The little girl lowered her arm and disappeared, taking the wind of bitterness and hunger with her as she left.

CHAPTER 4

Home Planet, Toronto, Canada

"YOU MUST BE DR. ADDAMS. I'm Susan. Please come in."

Jaguar stood on the front porch of the Karas house on Spodina Street as Susan Karas opened the door wide and extended an arm inward. Jaguar crossed the threshold into a wide entrance hall with a thick Persian rug laid over shiny white tiles. Expensive. The best.

She followed Susan into the living room and looked around. It was painted in neutral tones, with neutral furniture and beige satin curtains at the windows. Paintings of muted pastel flowers and family photos hung on the walls. The flowers in a crystal vase on the coffee table were fresh. The rug was thick and soft and clean. She'd read in the files that the Karas's had old money, through the father's family.

Mrs. Karas waved toward the deeply cushioned couch. "Please sit," she said.

"I appreciate your cooperation, Mrs. Karas," Jaguar said.

"Of course," she said, waving it away. "Anything—if it will help with this mess. It's awful. Oh, and do call me Susan."

Jaguar considered telling Susan to call her Jaguar, then sensed she wouldn't be comfortable using that name. It wouldn't go with the furniture, or her very expensive and neutral clothes. She was groomed as perfectly as her house, but Jaguar noted the fatigue lines at her eyes, the pinched flesh at her mouth. She was holding tight, trying to get through events nothing had ever prepared her for.

"It's been tough on all of you," Jaguar commented.

"Worst for Daro, of course. He can't go to school, so he's getting tutored through the courts, and the guard follows him everywhere. You were stopped by the one out in front?"

Jaguar nodded. A large man in a protective vest took her credentials. The Province was going to a lot of trouble to make sure Daro didn't die, or kill anyone in some embarrassing way, as the other boys had.

Susan sighed. "Everyone's been great, really protective. His guards, and his law guardian's wonderful, but Daro has to answer all these questions over and over again. And so do I. So does his father."

"What questions do they ask you?"

"Oh, why did we send him to Dr. Senci? Do we have any marital trouble?" She made a derisive sound. "Marital trouble. As if that explains why Daro—why any of this happened."

As if they were the criminals, Jaguar thought. Technically, anyone who reported sexual abuse was only a witness, acting properly as citizens to help the Province prosecute a crime, but Daro was inherently suspect because he'd gone to see a neuropsych specialist in the first place.

"Daro went to Dr. Senci for help with nightmares, didn't he?" Jaguar asked.

Susan confirmed this, but added that nightmares were too mild a word. He had wild, raging, terrifying dreams that woke him nightly and kept him up until daylight, when he could sometimes collapse into a few hours restless sleep. He stopped doing his homework, going to school, playing with friends.

His parents wanted to know if he was a candidate for Liratone, a new wonder drug for childhood Attention Deficit Disorder that had the unexpected benefit of giving beautiful, soothing dreams. They wanted the best for their son, and Dr. Senci was known as that, so they consulted with him. Dr. Senci's notes indicated his belief that Mr. and Mrs. Karas were somehow creating the nightmares. They were suspect from the minute they called him.

And for all Jaguar knew, they should be. She'd worked with enough pedophiles to know upper middle class white parents were not immune from that moral disaster. It was entirely possible that Daro, unable to accuse his parents, threw the blame onto the nearest available substitute. Jaguar had to consider that possibility. Of course, it didn't explain what happened to the other boys, but technically that was none of her business. She was here only to collect information on Daro and Dr. Senci.

The panel of judges they'd present their case to, borrowed from the Medical Protective Board, made a public fuss about their policy of zero tolerance for sexual abuse between doctor and patient, but the MPB also took care of its own, so Jaguar was also wary of them. She knew they'd agreed to a closed hearing, at the parent's request. She wondered if that was to shield Daro, or the doctor. Or maybe it was meant to shield the parents. This would wreak havoc on their social lives, Jaguar thought.

Mr. Karas was in banking, and had a social circle where this sort of thing wasn't mentioned. Mrs. Karas worked part-time in an art gallery, a pretty career for the wife of a banker. Of course, Daro's name had been kept out of the press, and so Jaguar supposed they could still hide their involvement from some people, but if the trial was public, that would be all over.

"Dr. Senci was treating the boys involved in the shooting, correct?" Jaguar asked.

"Yes. Also for nightmares. Daro talked to one of them in the waiting room. They—they got to be friends. The other boy—John DeLucas—Daro didn't know."

"Did you get a diagnosis for Daro from another doctor?" Jaguar asked.

"Two. Good thing it was all covered. They went over him head to toe. They both said they wouldn't have prescribed the liratone. Nothing wrong with him except—PTSD, they said."

"Post-traumatic stress disorder," Jaguar said. The cluster of problems someone develops when they've been traumatized and haven't integrated or healed the traumatic events. PTSD was assumed in her prisoners, and then specific syndromes diagnosed. What fear couldn't they integrate? Why not? Did they need medication as well as intervention? She'd have to see Daro's files to find out if the doctors had gotten any more specific.

"That's right. I remember I was just relieved he wasn't *born* with anything wrong. I guess I worry," Susan admitted.

"He's your only child, isn't he?"

"One I never thought I'd have. Even with the *in vitro*, I had a hard time going to term. I keep thinking—"

She paused, and Jaguar filled in the blanks for her.

"If only you didn't have that glass of wine while you were pregnant. If only you were younger. If only you took more vitamins. And what about great uncle Harry who never was quite right. Like that?"

Susan shook her head. "Stupid, isn't it?"

"Normal is a better word, I think."

"Well," she said uncertainly. "Maybe. Would you like something to drink? Coffee, or something cold maybe? And a little food?"

"Coffee would be wonderful, if it isn't any trouble. Shuttle coffee's the worst."

"No trouble at all," she said.

They were moving toward the kitchen when the front door swung open wide and then slammed shut hard. Jaguar turned, and saw a small-ish boy in sleeveless net shirt and shorts, baseball cap turned around backwards on his head, a gold hoop earring with a growling tiger dangling from the end of it in his left ear.

She found herself grinning. He could have been any child, from any age, except for the blinking electronic earcuff clipped over the tiger earring, which would allow him to communicate with his guards from anywhere. He scowled, removed it and laid it down on the table by the door before it was done blinking.

"Daro," his mother said reprovingly, "aren't you supposed to keep that in all the time?"

"Why? I mean, I can't go anywhere except the yard and the stupid courthouse, and the guy's always right there. And now I'm just *here*." He stopped himself, and knit his brow at Jaguar. "Who's she?" he asked, pointing.

She walked over to him, keeping her grin under control. "I'm Dr. Addams," she said, extending a hand.

She saw his instinctive withdrawal. Another doctor, here to poke and prod at him.

"Not that kind of doctor," she said quickly. "It's an academic title. It means I went to school for too long. You can call me Jaguar."

His face shifted its expression to interest. When he wasn't scowling he seemed younger. Those eyes, open wide enough to let in the whole world, too wide to keep out danger.

"Jaguar?" he asked. "Like those big cats? They're extinct."

"Actually," she said, "There's still some left in captivity. Not too far from here, at a place called Exotic Cat World, off the 401."

"Superhype," he said. "You mean that? Hey mom, you hear that? Maybe we could go?"

"We'll see," she said. "I'll talk to your father about it."

He grinned, lopsided. Mothers, his face said. Then he pushed his hand out to her, and she took it. "Are you, like, a lawyer?"

"Not even close."

"Cop?"

"Not that either. I'm a Teacher on the Planetoids."

His eyes widened with respect. The general public didn't really know much about those bits of glowing light floating above them, but they understood the work there was dangerous. The rest they filled in with their own imaginings.

"What're you here for?" he asked.

"Daro," his mother said, "A little politeness, please."

"I wasn't impolite," he said. "I just asked."

"That's fine," Jaguar agreed. "Always ask when you want to know something. I'm here to collect preliminary information on Dr. Senci for Planetoid research, in case he ends up there." She paused a moment. "And I'm here to help you. You did a brave thing, getting that recording on Dr. Senci. You deserve some help."

Officially, that wasn't true. And officially, it wasn't protocol. She wasn't supposed to help. But she'd come here to do just that. That much she knew already.

His face grew sober and concerned. She could see the places where his childhood would drop from his cheeks and the bones live close to the flesh. He would be a handsome young man.

"It wasn't brave," he said. "I just didn't want to have to, like, *explain* what happened. Besides I knew cops need evidence. Right?"

She nodded. "You did the right thing."

"You gonna ask me a lot of questions about the other boys?"

"Not too many," Jaguar said. "I'm here about you, not them."

"I can tell you something," he said firmly. "I know why they did it. Shot people."

"Why?"

"Because he said to. And I know why they killed themselves."

"Why?" Jaguar asked softly.

"Because they didn't want to become him," Daro said. Fear made his face young again, a little boy seeking shelter from madmen.

She saw herself at his age, living in the streets, her hands covered with blood from the rats she'd catch and eat, her eyes a wall against everything. Then, as if someone had changed channels on a television, she saw Daro kneeling in front of Dr. Senci, whose face stretched into sexual ecstasy while Daro's eyes were blank with horror. She saw him struggle to be released from the Doctor's hand, heard him gasp.

Stop it. That feels funny.

Just a little more, Daro. Good boy. That's the way.

Jaguar stepped back, and the image dissolved. They hadn't made contact. At least, she hadn't. What had she seen? She took in air, a short breath sucked in between her teeth. Daro, looking at her, shuddered.

Susan put a hand on his shoulder. "Daro?" she asked.

He shrugged, but leaned into her at the same time.

"We don't have to talk about lawyers and trials just yet, do we?" Susan turned to Jaguar and smiled hard. "Let's have a snack, and Daro, you should change and wash up for dinner. Let's do that. Okay?"

Jaguar turned to her. She was desperately seeking a way to keep this tidy and clean. And she hadn't a chance in hell of succeeding.

"I think that would be a very good idea," Jaguar said, and followed her to the kitchen.

Planetoid Three—Toronto Replica, Zone 12

The day after Jaguar left for Toronto Alex went back to the Senci file, and a hard copy of Davidson's *Etiquette of Vampires*. He opened the book and the file on his desk, and contemplated.

Dr. Senci's file was merely a review of the basic facts. After the Serials his primary home was in Toronto, though he maintained his New York residence. He had money he said came from his family, but those records were destroyed in the violence, so they couldn't check on that.

Looting, mugging, searching the pockets of the dead—all this was common during the Killing Times, though Dr. Senci didn't seem the type for that kind of thuggery.

Alex drummed his fingers on his desk and peeked at his computer screen to check his calendar for the day. Final reports to file. Stats to update. He had training sessions all day tomorrow, something he often brought Jaguar to. Training was the best time to get to know new Teachers and to spot the ones with psi capacities. Jaguar could sniff those out even before the Teacher knew they had them, and given her own skills, she was the best at showing them how to use what they had.

She carefully couched all her words in psychological terminology because the Governor's Board still frowned on open use of the empathic arts, but they knew her, so they must know what she was up to. Probably they'd use it against her the next time she got in trouble, though at this point he didn't think they'd fire her. She'd prevented too many potential PR disasters for them to risk that. They'd keep her around, because they never knew when they'd need her.

He didn't think they'd be so lenient if they knew she was researching vampires, subspecies Greenkeepers. He wasn't sure what he thought of it himself.

He stroked the book on his desk, flipped the pages around while he mentally reviewed the basics. Davidson said Greenkeepers accessed regenerative biochemicals through energy, blood or sex. She saw it as a specific psi capacity, and since it allowed them to live virtually forever, they had plenty of time to develop expertise in other psi capacities as well. They were usually hypnopaths and Telekines as well, often shapeshifters or Protean changers. If they were empaths, they would also be deeply shadowed, filled with that emptiness extant from the beginning of time.

They were a dissonance, Davidson said, in a universe that strived toward harmony. A gathered bundle of negative energy moving outside the constraints of time. The longer they lived and fed, the more energy they could accrue, and the more energy they accrued, the longer they continued to live and feed.

Davidson said their energy field appeared either as a space emptied of light or a dense greyness, but unless you knew that, you could stand next to one on the streets and notice nothing unusual beyond a slight but constant chill. An empath might sicken in their presence, or catch an odor of decaying flesh in their breath, said to be mildly toxic.

If one fed off you once or twice the results would be nausea, flu-like aches and weakness, but if they kept feeding off you, you'd wither and die unless you became a Greenkeeper and fed off someone else. And only a Greenkeeper could transform someone who was not born to it, something they rarely did since they weren't big on sharing.

She speculated that perhaps there was actually only one original Greenkeeper, a mutation that never spread because it would not serve the human species well. That template may have made others in its early days, then seen the folly of overpopulating the planet with more like itself. And it might still be alive.

Destroying any Greenkeeper was difficult at best since they could regenerate and heal wounds rapidly. If you shot a Greenkeeper once, odds were high you wouldn't live long enough to get in a second shot, or to plunge your hand into his chest to rip his heart out, one of the best ways to kill them. They were, Davidson added by way of exquisite understatement, highly dangerous.

That is, they were dangerous if they existed, which Davidson never admitted to believing. In fact, she stated frankly that there was no evidence backing any of the stories she'd collected. Nor, Alex thought, did any of it necessarily have anything to do with Dr. Senci, though Jaguar obviously suspected it might. Still, she had yet to say the magic words, Dr. Senci is a Greenkeeper, and she wouldn't until she knew they were true. She was proceeding more slowly than usual, and he was glad of that.

A knock on his door brought his attention away from his reading. "Come in," he said, and the door opened to Rachel, who walked in and handed him a disk.

"Senci," she said. "Or actually, it's about his victim. His psych evaluation. I couldn't get it until we were officially on the case."

Alex slid the disc into his computer. Rachel stood behind his chair, looking over his shoulder. The file scrolled out the medical life of Daro Karas, born twelve years ago to an older couple in Toronto, through the aid of in vitro fertilization. His infancy was normal. His toddler-hood was normal. He'd had all his vaccinations, grew at the usual pace, got all his teeth in, and showed no signs of ill health. A fine and healthy male specimen.

Then, at eleven, he started having nightmares, in a specific and repetitive form. They got so bad his parents took him to see his doctor, who recommended Dr. Senci.

Alex knew all this. Then, something on line three caught his eye. He read, then twisted a scowling face to Rachel. "Hell. Did she know this?" he asked.

Rachel shook her head. "She won't get this until tomorrow, when she meets with the Provincial people. And it's kind of buried so she might not catch it right away. I mean, that wording—metaphoric interpolations involve mythic creatures, etcetera. That's why I brought it up. So you could let her know."

Alex leaned away from his computer. Another room to add to this house of horrors.

The jargon of psychology translated into something quite simple. Daro dreamt, constantly and virulently, of vampires.

Home Planet, Toronto, Canada

"Thank you, child," Dr. Senci said. "You did a good job for me."

The little girl shifted from one foot to the other. She wasn't sure which was worse—when he was nice to her, or when he was angry. At least when he was angry she knew to stay away. When he was nice she didn't know what to expect. "Can I go?" she asked.

"No," he said. "There's more for you to do. Come here."

He crooked a finger at her, drawing her toward the deep upholstered chair he sat in next to the fire. Of all his houses, she liked this one best. It had a fireplace, and she liked fire. When he wasn't around, she'd burn things in it, watching flames lick at old books, at paper, at his shirts. Everything burned different, she learned. Each burning had its own look, its own smell and feel.

Often he left the children alone, either here or at his house in New York. Sometimes she'd be in charge, and sometimes Peter would. She didn't like that much. Peter was bossy. The oldest of the children and almost ready to transform, he liked to pretend he was Dr. Senci. If he got too bossy she'd kick him or gouge at his eyes, but he was bigger and hard to beat. Still, he was better than Dr. Senci, who never left her alone.

She approached his chair slowly, reluctantly. When she was within reach he grabbed her by the neck, pulled her between his legs and held her pinioned.

"You will be my eyes and ears. My little angel. You will draw her to us," he crooned.

"Leggo," she said, pushing against him.

"Not yet," he said. "This is very important, and you must listen. Unless—perhaps you've changed your mind and you don't want a mother?"

She was still. He'd had her for three years and it took two of them for him to find her pressure point. She did not respond to violence or bribes, but one night he caught her mooning over one of her storybooks about princesses and fairy godmothers, and found out that more than anything, she wanted a mother. Not like her own mother, who sold her to him for a dose of latrinol. She wanted a real mother.

"Do you want a mother, angel?" he asked.

"Don't call me that," she said. "I don't like it."

"I wouldn't, if you'd tell me what your name is," he said.

She shook her head. Nobody knew her name. Nobody was going to, either, except maybe her real mother. He relaxed his legs, and she slipped out from between them, backed up quickly and stood just outside of his reach.

"Come back here, my angel," he cajoled.

She stamped a small foot on the carpet. "*Don't* call me that. I can't be an angel because I'm not dead."

Dr. Senci didn't laugh. He never laughed at her unless he had her pinned down so that she couldn't bite or scratch because she'd do both. She was the youngest of his pack, and the most fierce. If she lived to adulthood she might become an interesting companion, or perhaps a good feed. Right now, she was a powerful and ill-tempered brat, very gifted in the empathic arts, but with no direction in her use of them.

"Keep this up, and you will be. I'll take you back to Manhattan and leave you there for the rats to eat."

She lifted her leg and kicked him hard, and when he reached for her, she bared her teeth to bite. He got hold of her wrists with one hand and dangled her in the air away from him while she wiggled and screeched. He dropped her and twisted her wrist.

You'll do what I say, or you'll die.

Suddenly, she ceased struggling. Leaned back on her haunches and relaxed.

"I'm tired," she whined. "I don't want to."

Something like a sob caught in her throat. Dr. Senci brought his hand back and slapped her hard. She fell flat onto her back and lay there, water welling up in her eyes. That wasn't good. Both the chemical combination of salt water and the specific energy in the emotion of sorrow were physically painful to him and he tolerated no pain. No interference with his pleasure.

No crying. Don't play with me or I'll fuck you until you're dead.

Her face tightened into stillness.

"Get up," he said out loud. "And come over here."

She rubbed at her cheek and did as she was told in sullen silence.

He pulled her into his lap. "If you want a mother, you must do this, tired or not. I'll help you get ready." He held her shoulders and felt her sigh as she settled into the work at hand.

He'd never taught her how to leave her body. She already knew how, and used it to escape him the first time he tried to sex her. Just as he was ready to take her she went flying out from herself and across the room.

When he grabbed for her she threatened to go out the window and into a flock of white birds that flew overhead.

Pigeons. She would fly with pigeons rather than be with him. He found that insulting, considering the situation he'd rescued her from—a wastrel child with no future, living with her addict mother and a group of dying druggies. When he bought her she was filthy and malnourished, but good food and adequate shelter soon brought her back to health and a bounding energy. Then the ungrateful wretch left her body every time he tried to sex her. Finally he decided to use her skills in ways that suited him.

She became his messenger. His little angel. He taught her how to direct her travels over greater distances, and now she could appear as a ghostlike figure wherever he sent her. If all went as he planned she'd help bring him the woman they both sought, but she made such a fuss about it he'd almost made up his mind to kill her once she'd gotten him what he wanted. She had limited usefulness, and apparently unlimited trouble in her.

Sometimes he killed the children at the moment they expected to be transformed, slashing their throats and letting their blood pour into his hands before he fed. He'd make the other children watch. It increased their respect and let him drink their fear, allowing him to experience the terror of death the only way he could—vicariously.

Perhaps this little girl who bit would give him that thrill someday. Now she had work to do for him. He pressed a hand against her forehead, felt her readiness to begin.

"There, my little angel," he said. "Go out and play. The Jaguar is waiting to see you."

CHAPTER 5

Home Planet—Toronto, Canada

JAGUAR'S HOTEL WAS OUTSIDE THE CITY, in an area called Scarborough, cynically referred to as Scarberia because of the empty malls that made jagged scars along the road. From her 11th story room she could scan the carcasses of abandoned consumerism scattered at her feet.

When she was done paying her respects in that quarter she turned to her telecom and punched in the code she knew best. She waited, and then smiled when Alex's angular face appeared on screen. They'd traded messages back and forth since her arrival but they hadn't actually managed to speak. He hadn't made empathic contact, but in the moments before she fell asleep she had a distinct sense of his presence. Just a kiss at the back of her neck, and then a departure.

"Miss me?" she asked lightly.

He turned a hand over, inclined his head, gestures which said of course, and since when was that news. "How's it going?" he asked.

"Interesting. I'm spending time with Daro."

"And what do you say about him?"

"Maxxed out PTSD. Other than that, he's a great kid. Parents conservative, wealthy, keeping up appearances. Pure Toronto."

"Mm-hm. Did they confirm that Daro's nightmares were about vampires?"

She missed a beat. "You know about that?"

He turned a hand over, inclined his head. Same gesture. Same meaning. Of course he knew. "Learn anything else?" he asked.

She shifted in her seat, then closed her eyes and leaned back. Her thoughts ran into his. Just feelings. Something old and cold and empty. An absence of heart. A dank grey nothing.

"Like that," she said, opening her eyes. "It's very . . . " she let the sentence dissipate.

He leaned in and looked at her eyes. The small lines around them, the circles underneath. Shadows moved through the green and gold of her iris, taking the light out of them.

"Have you been in empathic contact with Daro?" he asked.

"No. Why?"

He looked harder. Whatever he'd seen was gone, like a shadow that shifted and left the day clear. "Don't. Not yet. Did you interview Senci yet?"

"Later today," she said.

"Maybe you should delay that," he suggested,

"Is that the Adept speaking?" she asked.

He shook his head. He wasn't sure. The Adept, or the man who pointed his scissors down when he ran. The man who was courting her. "Just be careful. Make no contact, and don't try any of your tricks. That's an order from your Supervisor."

Her mouth curled into a smile. "Since when has that ever worked?"

"Never. But it's all I've got, so I use it."

"No, Alex," she contradicted. "You've got plenty you could use. You're just too much of a gentleman to do so. And I appreciate that."

She signed off, watching his face disappear into darkened screen.

When he was gone, she rubbed at her temples. She needed more sleep. She was waking repeatedly from disjointed dreams. Alex was in them, and her knife, and ugly laughter, but she couldn't remember anything else. She breathed in and out. Then she stood, and prepared to leave.

* * * *

Riding the glass elevator down from her room to the lobby, Jaguar could see the Maggie—local name for the electromag subway line—curving against the outlines of the city like a silver vein. The tall glass buildings changed shades as the sun shifted in the sky. At night the lights of the city flickered at her feet while she rode down the side of the moon toward earth.

Jaguar liked to watch the city rise to meet her, as if she commanded this movement. It gave her the illusion that she had some control. But this Toronto was not her Planetoid Toronto, and nobody named Alex, nobody who was her friend, lived here. Instead, she rode the Maggie with people who wore subdued suits and worked hand-held computers. They were silent, and their eyes stayed put.

Toronto was hit hard by the Serials. It only appeared to have less trouble than New York or L.A. because they were so efficient at clearing away bodies. Some commentators said they lost more people than L.A., but were too determinedly polite to talk about it.

It was a city filled with clean light, catching sun in the glass and chrome spires of its buildings, and she didn't fit in at all. Twice on the Maggie people had changed seats to move away from her. They sensed her presence as a foreign substance, filled with sharp edges that frayed their smooth surfaces.

She kept her clothes to the most subdued and tailored she could find in her closet. She kept her hair knotted at her neck. She discarded the feathers she liked to wear, but the people who lived here knew she was a different energy among them. No matter how you dressed her up, she still smelled like Planetoid. Either that, or the mint she always carried with her.

As she rode downtown she reached into her jacket pocket and rubbed some between finger and thumb. The sweet sharp scent of mint, reminding her she was alive. She might need that. She was going to interview Senci.

The electromag stopped under the courthouse, and she ascended to it. Senci was out on bail, but he was required to wear a tracking implant, and to make himself available for any interviews the authorities wanted. The courts provided her with a room and a guard, even a laser fence between them, for her interviews.

A woman in uniform whose round face matched her round figure sat at the front desk, staring at a computer. "May I help you?" she asked without looking away from it.

Jaguar showed her papers. "Here to interview Dr. Senci."

The woman glanced briefly at them, then looked again a little harder. She lifted her head up and took a good stare at Jaguar. "Planetoid?" she asked.

"Like it says," she admitted.

The woman wrinkled her nose, then chewed on her lip. "I'm thinking of leaving here. What's it like up there?"

"Different," Jaguar said. "Very different."

The woman asked no further questions. She called to a guard, who led her down the hall and up a flight of stone steps to a featureless grey interview room. The guard seated her at a table where the laser fence was up and humming. Under normal circumstances, she would have insisted on working without it. Today, she was glad it was there.

Not many minutes passed before the door opened and Senci stepped inside. She blinked hard because she couldn't see him clearly. He seemed to dissolve, to fall into the air as if he was part of it. It took her a long moment to realize she was seeing his energy field, a dense grey. She shifted her focus as he sat at the table across from her, working hard to keep him in her eyes because he had a tendency to disappear into the grey of the walls.

He smiled, at ease and unafraid. His sharp blue eyes were focused and keenly aware of his surroundings. "Hello, Jaguar," he said.

He knew her name. Had his lawyer told him? Probably. But his voice. Something in his voice. As he spoke her ears were ringing and light ringed her pupils. She gathered herself together and spoke. "You know my name. Do you know why I'm here?"

His answer came subvocally, a shock within her.

I know why you think you're here Jaguar I know more than that Jaguar I know I know do you?

She couldn't see him through the cloud of dense grey around him, and her ears were ringing. She turned her face down to the file resting on the table. Better. That was better.

"I'm here to conduct a standard interview for Planetoid records," she said, keeping her voice official, professional, keeping her eyes off his face. "There's a series of questions we routinely ask, so I'll ask them, and you'll answer. Or, you can choose not to answer, and I'll mark that down. Ready?"

She raised her face to his, caught a glimpse of it before it was swallowed in cloud.

Do you know what I am Jaguar Jaguar Jaguar do you?

She looked away again. He was definitely a hypnopath, and a good one. But she could deal with that. Good blocking techniques and a refusal of their tricks worked just fine with them. She referred to the file. "Have you ever been abused, sexually or physically?" she asked.

You should know, you of all people should see it marked clearly do you?

"Right," she said. "No answer. Do you drink or take any drugs?"

Even if you don't I'm glad you're here there is so much we have to talk about so much we have to do.

She stared at the file, at the questions she still had to ask. As if any of them would tell her what she needed to know. Ridiculous. Pencil pusher crap. She could think of only one question that might help her, whether he answered or not.

She raised her eyes, trying to peer around what hid him.

"What are you after?" she asked.

You'll know in time and time is a funny thing isn't it Jaguar but it isn't time yet so you must be patient.

"What the hell does that mean?" Her voice was slow and watery, pouring from her throat like blood.

Answers will come in time but now you must leave. You must leave. You must leave.

Time was a funny thing, here in this clouded place. It took a long time, it seemed, for her to rise. Geological ages passed while she pressed her hands into the table and lifted herself from her chair. Planets were born and died as she turned from the table and walked across the room.

Then, within the speed of light, she was out the door and standing on the street, blinking up at bright sunlight.

"Eldest brother," she whispered. "What the hell was that?"

* * * *

Jaguar walked Yonge for more than an hour, finding her way into the various markets and just standing and smelling foods, touching fruits and vegetables piled on carts, looking hard at her own feet. She wanted physical contact with solid material goods. She stood in front of an Indian Food Supply store and breathed in. Fennel and peppers and cardamom and unidentified sharpness filled her, and gradually she came back to herself.

She had to be at the Karas house for dinner in half an hour, but she didn't rush the process. She didn't want them to see anything wrong with her. She didn't want them to ask questions she couldn't answer, because what did she know except that Dr. Senci was using the arts? Using them expertly, with purpose.

Standing under bright sun, the sharp scent of cardamom and cumin all around, the nightmare sense she'd felt with him was fading. She took a moment to evaluate her experience.

Clearly, Senci was a hypnopath, and a very good one, deeply shadowed. She could smell that on him a mile away. And clearly he had an agenda beyond the trial, but what else he was and what agenda he hoped to fulfill were still very much not clear.

She'd seen a grey field around him, but that could be hypnopath trickery, all showmanship. Smoke in mirrors, quite literally. A good hypnopath could easily create that to scare a vulnerable audience. Still, she understood Daro's reaction to him. To a young boy already plagued by nightmares, creepy wouldn't begin to describe it. But she could help Daro deal with a shadowed hypnopath.

She'd give him a few tips for blocking his moves. She thought he'd respond well. There wasn't much empath in him, but he was a good kid, with more guts than most. And he had an innate sense of how to protect his privacy, create safe space for himself. Susan had showed her the shed in their well-groomed backyard, which she called Daro's workshop.

Jaguar asked Daro about it and he shrugged, "I make things sometimes. You know."

She took that to mean the shed was his private space, no admittance. She didn't press him on it. In fact, she made it a point not to press him on anything, which he seemed to appreciate. She could tell he was expecting her to ask more questions about the trial, about Dr. Senci, about how he felt. When she didn't, he would shrug into himself and ask if she wanted to play catch, or a computer game. If she said yes, his whole body would breathe out relief.

She shook herself, and turned away from the Indian store. She knew a few more things, and she could move forward with Daro. That was good. Now she should try and get to dinner on time.

She took the electromag to the Karas home, was admitted inside and went first to the living room. Halfway across the thick beige carpet, she stopped.

Daro was sitting on the long white couch, head down, kicking his legs against the bottom wood strip just below the upholstery.

"What's wrong?" she asked.

He scowled briefly, and ducked his head back down.

Jaguar crossed the carpet, kicked off her sandals and sat down next to him. She didn't know what to say, so she waited. That's what her grandmother had done for her when she was young and couldn't find words to circumscribe her moods.

The moment of her birth was the moment of her mother's death and so her grandparents had raised her. At first they lived in New Mexico, where she felt the hot sun on her back, the stones soft and gritty under her feet as she listened to the adults drum and sing in their village of 13 Streams. But that only lasted until she was five. Then her grandparents moved to Manhattan, where her grandfather filled one of the first UN representative seats for Native Americans.

When she turned eleven, the Serials began. Before she turned twelve her grandparents were dead and she was tossed into the streets to seek survival on her own.

That was her childhood. It was about the extremes. Death and life. Abundance and starvation. Freedom and entrapment. The beauty of the mesa, and the ugliness of the human spirit in fear. Terror and escape from terror. How to kill, and how to avoid being killed. The power of the empath, and the powerlessness of a child in the midst of death.

And it occurred to her that Daro's childhood was like hers. He moved between his parents carefully nurtured security and the world of Dr. Senci. She took in a breath and let it out.

"You want to tell me about it?" she asked.

"No. Yes. I don't know." He kicked the couch some more.

"Well, is it something embarrassing, about a girl or something?"

He wrinkled his nose as if he smelled something bad. "Girls?"

"Maybe not. Then is it something to do with the trial?"

"No," he said, "and it's not that interesting."

"Okay," she said. "But I feel bad, seeing you feel bad. So I'm trying to find out if I can do anything to help."

He frowned, then turned a grin toward her. "That's what my parent's always do, isn't it?"

"Probably," she said. "I don't have much experience with parents, so I'm only guessing."

He thought about this, then asked, "Where are your parents?"

"They died when I was a baby. My grandparents raised me, and they're... also dead." She wondered how specific she should be. She settled for plain facts. "They were murdered during the Serials," she said.

"Oh," he said, adding politely, "I'm sorry. You don't have any kids?"

She shook her head. "No kids. No husband."

"You're not married?" he asked. "Why not?"

She smiled wryly. "It never came up."

He blushed, then wiped at his face to hide the color on his cheeks.

"Now that you know all my secrets," she said, "tell me what's bothering you."

"Nothing. Just—Mom won't let me try out for Little League."

"Oh. Why not?"

"She thinks—someone might find out. About me and Dr. Senci."

Jaguar's forehead creased in thought. "I guess you can't play until the trial's over, right?"

"Yeah, but I could try out. They just don't want anybody to know."

She ran a hand through her hair. "They're afraid," she said. "But you haven't done anything wrong. You know that, right?"

He hunched his shoulders and said nothing.

"It's the same as if you were robbed. It's not your fault, and the trial isn't about you. Really, you're just a witness to the crime."

"That's what the lawyer says. Clara. "

"She's right, but I suppose it doesn't feel like that to you." She would have said more, but she heard Susan clearing her throat. She looked up and saw her standing in the arched doorway between livingroom and kitchen, her face written with anger and bitter shame. She worked to overcome it, which Jaguar appreciated.

"Daro," she said, "Dr. Addams is right. It's not your fault. I don't—I never meant you to feel that. Do you understand? Do you?"

Though she was quite still, to Jaguar, it seemed as if her whole body wanted to propel forward to her son. He hunched back into himself. "Yeah, I know Mom," he said.

A sharp sensation of how far away they all were from each other caught Jaguar between the ribs. This, followed by the deeper grief of knowing she would probably only make that worse.

"S'time to eat yet?" Daro asked.

"Wash your hands first," his mother said, "and don't forget to use soap."

* * * *

Jaguar sat kitty-corner to Philip Karas at dinner, which was conducted at a table set with fine bone china and silver, the proper number of forks, spoons, and glasses. It made Jaguar nervous that she'd spill something, and she could see Daro watching her, chewing back on a grin when her hand moved to the wrong utensil. Except for a very brief introduction over the telecom, all her contact had been with Susan and Daro. Philip was the absence in their lives, and in Jaguar's picture of their lives together. She hadn't yet ruled him out as a suspect in Daro's abuse, but meeting him would settle that.

He spoke easily and with intelligence about the philosophy of crime, quoting Foucault and Teresian. He was smart, well-read, liked to show off a little, and lived mostly in his head. Brief scans of his interior showed her nothing more dangerous than a need to stay on top of things, an attachment to superiority of intellect. As he spoke she also kept herself tuned to Daro's signals, searching for any distress. So far, there was only the normal father-son tension.

"And how do you place the Planetoid's work in terms of Foucault's paradigm, Dr. Addams?" Philip asked.

Jaguar brought her attention back to her host. "Well outside his ken," she said, "It's not something he could imagine."

"But you hold ultimate power over your prisoners, don't you?"

"Only if they don't kill us," she said. Susan's face showed mild shock, and Jaguar smiled to lighten her words. This kind of intellectual discussion always brought out the bad in her. A need to jab and draw blood.

Philip nodded judiciously. "Pass the salt, please," he requested. She complied, managing not to knock over any glassware, but just barely. "But I think systems of punishment are in general heading toward extinction."

"I hope so," Jaguar said cheerfully.

Philip laughed. "Wouldn't you be out a job?"

"Not at all," she replied. "The Planetoids are rehabilitative. Redemptive. Not punitive."

"That's not what I heard," Daro interjected. "I heard they squish your head until all your brains fall out, then they put your brains through a— like a—"

"Supersquisher?" Jaguar asked. "Squeeze all the juice out and drink it?"

Daro made a face, grabbed his own throat and throttled himself.

"Daro," Susan reprimanded. "Not at the table."

He shrugged and went back to his food.

"Not anywhere," Philip said, shaking his head. Then he turned back to Jaguar. "He shouldn't be encouraged, Dr. Addams. His nightmares. We don't want them to recur."

Jaguar considered him. She wondered how he felt about what was happening to his son. He didn't seem the type to feel anything easily. Probably he'd think it first.

"Some experts say it's good for children to work out their fears through fantasy," she noted.

Philip shook his head. "There's a correlation between fantasy violence in the use of VR systems and increased rates of violence, detachment from reality in children."

Jaguar smiled. "You have a VR system, don't you?"

"For educational programs," Susan cut in. "All the latest in language, travel—even a woodworking program. Daro likes to work with wood. Ask him to show you his workshop in the shed. He's making a guitar, aren't you, Daro?"

"Mom," Daro said. "That's my business."

Jaguar smiled at him, then turned back to Philip. "Maybe it's different with stories. They seem to help children contain their fears, confront them in small doses. Emotions like that can't be denied. You have to deal with it, and direct it—appropriately."

Philip gave a small, polite smile. "And that's what you do on the Planetoids?"

"That's right," she said. "We're good at it, too. We've got a very low rate of recidivism."

"That's because you do that mind stuff, isn't it?" Daro chimed in. "You're empaths, right?"

"Daro," his father remonstrated, "don't be rude.

"I'm not. I saw it on the news once," he said, waving a fork around. "About empaths and how they get into your mind. The army's researching it. Psi capacities they call it, though."

"Daro," his father said more firmly. He pointed at the fork, which Daro lowered. "Let's not get over excited."

"I'm not excited," he protested. "I saw it on the news. How the army was researching it, and the Planetoids used it or somebody said they did. Then some guy got on and said that was a lie. Will you use it on him?"

Him. Jaguar turned to Daro, blinked. "On Dr. Senci?"

"Yeah," Daro said. He waved his fork up toward the ceiling. "When you get him up there. Or will you just put a stake through his heart?"

Susan drew in a quick sharp breath. Jaguar stayed with Daro. "Maybe we'll just squeeze him until he explodes," she said.

"Or blow him up?" Daro said.

"Mm. With a bicycle pump."

"Yeah, but you gotta put a stake in his heart first. Otherwise—you know. They come back."

They come back. She saw the fear dancing under his rage.

I don't want to become him won't become him won't become him.

"Are you afraid of that?" she asked him quietly. "You're afraid he'll come back, make you like him? A vampire."

"Stop it," Susan said sharply, then looked around apologetically. "I—I can't eat when you're talking about—about—"

Philip reached over and patted her hand. "Enough, Daro," he said. Daro scowled quietly, while his father turned to Jaguar.

"We're trying to get him over that vampire notion. It's obviously a metaphor. The only way he can explain his pain. We really shouldn't be talking about it now."

Daro brought his scowl into focus and aimed it at his father. "It's not a damn metaphor, and I want her to squeeze his guts out. I want her to *kill* him," he said, voice rising in pitch. "I want *somebody* to kill him."

"Daro, nobody's going to kill anybody," his father said reasonably.

"I *want* her to. I want him dead. It's the only way." He was shouting now, eyes wild with terror and rage. He stood, pointed at his father.

"Or *you. You* kill him. You've got a gun, Dad. You keep it in your desk drawer. I saw it. Why didn't you just shoot him? He's a *fucker*, and he fucked me. I'd shoot him, if it was my kid."

He swept his hand across the table, sent his plate flying into the wall where it crashed and shattered. A moment of absolute stillness. Then, breathing hard, he ran from the room.

Jaguar heard the sound of his door slamming shut. Susan lowered her face into her hands. Philip went pale and sat back.

"I'm sorry, Dr. Addams," he said.

"I'm not the one who needs an apology," she said.

His lips went tight. "Are you suggesting I owe Daro an apology? I didn't do anything wrong."

"Neither did he," she said softly. "Neither did he."

CHAPTER 6

SHE STOOD ON A MESA AND RAVENS CIRCLED HER, spiraling out of sky like leaves. They landed at her feet and became Senci, who picked at her hair with eager fingers. She drank cold air and stared into Alex's dark eyes, close to her. Close to her. She held up her red glass knife and let it fall into his chest. His eyes were clear and filled with victory. Her red glass knife plunged into his heart and his blood ran into his hand which he lifted to her lips before he fell and Senci laughed.

Drink, he whispered.

Senci laughed.

"It's a pretty clear-cut case, and the precedents indicate Dr. Senci's headed for the Planetoids," Law guardian Clara Trianos said.

Jaguar blinked, lifted her head and frowned at the dark, polished woman across the dark, polished conference table. The vision, remnant of a dream, dispersed, leaving a bad taste in her mouth. Clara regarded her mildly.

She and Chief Prosecutor for the Province Diana Richburg had called the meeting, a normal part of the protocol, but then they proceeded to natter on about facts she already knew. Her mind had drifted, and now she called it back to business.

"If it's so clear cut," she said, "why do you look so worried?"

Diana and Clara studied each other, then her. They'd both worked with Planetoid researchers in the past, but not with her. When she introduced herself to them their faces were closed like bathroom doors, and they exuded tension. Apparently, they'd not only heard of her, they didn't like what they'd heard.

"We're concerned for Daro," Diana said. "He won't be questioned by the attorneys, but he has to speak before the judges after they view his interview tape. Frankly, our only worry is that he'll bring up the vampire issue."

"Why?" Jaguar asked, and saw the exchange of glances again. "I mean," she amended, "isn't it normal for traumatized kids to do that sort of thing. Name their molesters as monsters."

Clara grew thoughtful. "Sure, but it's one of those things that could go either way—generate sympathy, or take a bite out of his credibility. His ability to distinguish between fantasy and reality is a big issue, something defense'll use against us. So he can say it, but we have to direct *how* he says it."

"But you have a recording of Senci admitting what he did. Seems to me Daro could say he's a purple elephant with bad breath if he wants."

Diana looked a little shocked at this, but Clara loosened up enough to grin. "You'd think so, right? The voxchip's our ace in the hole. I don't know if we'd make the case without that. But there'll be expert testimony about whether or not it's been tampered with. I want the witness to look as good as the recording."

"Won't there be testimony from other patients? The families of the boys who killed themselves?"

"Can't do it. Prejudicial."

Jaguar tapped a finger against the table. "Okay. So why am I here? Is there something you want me to do? Or maybe something you want me *not* to do?"

The two women avoided exchanging meaningful glances, but only just. "Dr. Addams," Diana said, "Your interest in this—is it other than preliminary research?"

"Of course not. Why do you ask?"

"You're a little different than the other researchers we've had in the past," Clara noted.

Jaguar looked across the table at her, at Diana.

"You haven't used any of the standard questionnaires for Senci or Daro and his family," Diana said, "And you've spent more time with Daro than researchers usually do. We didn't know if that was connected to—well, to other Planetoid interests, maybe about his nightmares, which we don't want to focus on."

She frowned. She was distinctly not getting it.

"In—psi capacities and so on," Diana added.

The light went on. "What? You think I'm here vampire hunting?"

Diana made mild protest and Clara bit her lip against a grin. Jaguar lifted a hand, palm up. "I'm here to do a job, counselors," she said. "Gather information for our files and, if I can, help a boy who's had a bad break. That's all."

The chief prosecutor cleared her throat. "Of course. Just—we wanted to make sure we're all on the same page. And we wondered about your incomplete interview with Dr. Senci."

That. They were right. It wasn't much of an interview. "I was getting a sense of him. I'll do a more complete work-up on the next go around."

Diana's sensor went off. She pressed it, and stood. "Excuse me," she said. "I wouldn't take this, except I'm waiting on a bit of news about a drug lord. Clara, you'll carry on?"

"Of course. Go on ahead, Diana."

She exited, and Jaguar waited for what was next.

Clara considered her. "My work day's about over. Let's get out of here and go find a beer."

* * * *

The bar they went to was old, dark, and occupied by regulars who knew the bartender by name. Jaguar approved. She stayed with small talk until they were settled with beers in hand.

"So," Clara said, going straight to the heart of the matter, "What is it about you?"

Jaguar gave her a slow smile. "I assume you mean that differently than the last man I dated."

"Way different. Especially since I got to watch your interview with Senci. We record them, you knew that?"

"No. If I did—"

"You were told, and if you had objections, they wouldn't have got you anywhere. So I've seen the tape, and I want to know why you didn't talk to the guy."

"What?"

"You enter the interview room and sit down. Dr. Senci smiles at you. Some time passes. You leave. The only thing you do is get your pupils dilated, though I don't know if anyone besides me noticed that."

"I did better than that," she said. "Apparently it didn't record. You guys check your equipment?"

"All the time. It's working fine."

Jaguar sipped her beer meditatively. That was interesting. "What do you make of that?" she asked.

"I don't know yet," Clara said pointedly. "You've never done a prelim, right?"

"This is my first," she admitted.

"Your job on the Planetoid—you're called a Teacher, correct? Work directly with prisoners, take 'em through the hoops."

"That's right."

"I'd like to know why you took this on."

"Maybe," Jaguar said, "I wanted the experience."

Clara shook her head. "My mother didn't raise no fool. There's something else going on. And maybe it's okay, but whatever it is, I want in."

In the mirror hanging behind the bar, Jaguar saw a flick of motion. A small shadow. She turned. The little girl stood near a booth, her shoulder braced against a post. The people in the booth drank beer, ate peanuts, unaware of her presence.

Clara swiveled her seat around and looked where Jaguar was looking. "Someone you know?" she asked.

The girl brought her hand up to her mouth and giggled behind it. Her image shimmered, and disappeared.

"No," Jaguar said. "I thought so, but no. Listen, about Daro's vampire obsession—do *you* think he's delusional?" she asked. Fishing. Fishing for Clara's real side.

Clara ran a finger along the frost at the edge of her beer mug. "I think he's using the most apt metaphor he has. Vampires prey on the young. So does Dr. Senci. So do all pedophiles."

"I know," Jaguar said. "I work with them. On the Planetoids."

"Yeah. I read your files. It's a specialty."

Jaguar shrugged. "I specialize in the highly vexed. Pedophiles fit that bill. And you're right about them. They choose children as victims because they're afraid to die, afraid of anything more powerful than they are. Then, their victims often either ruin their own lives and die, or go on to become pedophiles themselves. You're right. It's like vampires."

She sipped her beer while Clara watched her and said nothing. Jaguar looked at her face in the mirror. She was intelligent and attentive. She wanted to hear what Jaguar had to say, but she had some theory of her own going, Jaguar thought. She was here, as Jaguar was, trying to confirm what she already thought was true.

"Have you spent time with Senci?" Jaguar asked.

"His lawyer won't let me anywhere near. But I had a long talk with the cop who did his initial questioning."

Something there, Jaguar thought. Something Clara didn't like. "And?" she asked.

"He came to talk to me about it privately, because it creeped him out. Said he wanted to give me the heads up, since I'm Daro's lawyer. He's from Manhattan, right? Refugee from the Killing Times, and he saw—well, he saw enough to give him good instincts about bad shit. And he was scared of Senci. Thought he was some kind of monster. Said he used words he remembered from the Killing Times and hadn't heard since."

"Like what?"

"He talked about sexing children. About feeding. About using them to—to—"

"Stay green?" Jaguar suggested.

Clara blinked in surprise. "Yeah. Those were the words. How did you know that?"

"I'm from Manhattan, too," she said, reminding herself to stay calm. It was more evidence, but not yet proof. Senci clearly liked to play with people, and that's all it might be. If he knew the stories about Greenkeepers he'd use the right words to scare a child, a cop. On the other hand, Clara was telling her she had more than ample proof of his legal guilt.

"But if he said that to a cop, doesn't that constitute a confession? And you record the interviews."

"Yeah. The disc got warped."

"Warped?"

"Well, really, it sort of melted down. Nobody knows why. And the transcript somehow got itself lost."

Jaguar frowned. "Can't the cop testify?"

"Not in his current condition. He's—existentially challenged."

"What?"

"He was hit by a cab the day after I talked to him. He's brain dead. On machines. The doctors don't know if he'll ever come out of it. I can't testify, because it's hearsay, and from checking around, he didn't tell anyone else the same things he told me."

Jaguar let the pieces fall into their proper place. None of this was in the file. Of course, it wasn't, because they couldn't use it. No valid evidence remained.

"Didn't the cops re-interview?" she asked.

"Sure, and Senci sang a whole different song. He denied everything, with a big long explanation of why Daro thought he was a vampire, and how that related to his general delusional neuroses and so on. The words got bigger as he went along. Said he suspected one of Daro's parents molested him. Shit like that. I'll say this for our Dr. Senci, he talks a good game."

Hell, Jaguar thought. He's not only playing with us, he's winning.

"I'll tell you what, though," Clara continued, "what that cop said— I'm not sure where to go with it. I mean, he was a real down-to-earth guy, no nonsense about him, and he said Senci was the scariest guy he ever met. That when he talked, the room went cold, and—and he smelled like death. That it was hard to breathe just sitting there with him. He said a lot of things. Then, he walked out in front of a cab and got brain dead. I didn't know what to think. I still don't."

"And no one else listened to the recording?"

"Nobody. He sealed it up and had the messenger take it to the Provincial Attorney's office. When they took it out, it looked like someone set fire to it."

"Like my interview?"

"Your disc was good, and at least with you we got a picture. Makes you look a little crazy, sister," she noted. "My boss—she's not sure she wants to be alone with you on a crowded city street."

"And you?" Jaguar asked.

Clara narrowed her dark eyes, squint lines appearing at the corners. "You might be crazy," she said. "But I don't think you're a liar. That's just my gut reaction."

Jaguar drained her beer and put the glass on the bar. Clara, floundering in water that ran too deep for her, was seeking help. Jaguar called the bartender over.

"I want tequila," she said to him, "but I'd like it to be good tequila. What's in stock?" He gave her the list, and she picked one. When he brought it, with lime and a shaker of salt, Jaguar set herself up properly and raised the shotglass to Clara.

"Gut reactions," she said, and threw it back.

Clara waited for the tequila shiver to run through her and settle down before she spoke. "Okay," she said. "So tell me who you are, and what's going on here, because I think you know."

Jaguar ran a finger around the bottom of her shotglass and licked it. She leaned forward and touched Clara on the forehead, spoke into her.

This is who I am.

One word appeared in Clara's mind.

Brujah. Witch.

Claro, Jaguar replied. *Yo Brujah.*

Clara pulled back, broke the connection. "Jesus. What the—"

"C'mon, Clara," Jaguar said out loud. "You read my files, you and your boss. I saw the looks. Bad enough having Planetoid researchers hanging around a case but for fuck's sake an empath, too."

"Yeah," Clara said, eyeing her. "Empaths who blow up shuttles and have a rep for coloring way outside the lines. At least, that's the rumors, and your board guy Paul Dinardo ain't denying them."

"Christ," Jaguar groaned. "You talked to him?"

"Well, your supervisor's good looking, but he's not giving anything away. Even Dinardo didn't *say* you're an empath. He just implied it. With a hammer."

"He's correct," Jaguar said. "I'm an empath. With a hammer."

"Right," Clara said. "And I'm not. Not that I have anything against it, mind you. I mean, my grandmother used to consult, and she always learned what she needed to know. But I don't want Daro used for anyone's game."

"Too late for that," Jaguar said. "Senci's already using him. But I'm not. I'm here to help."

"Then what do you know?"

"I know," Jaguar said carefully, "That Dr. Senci isn't—" how to finish that sentence. Isn't human. Isn't the regular run of the mill pedophile. "Isn't normal," she concluded lamely.

"Well, I could've told you that," Clara said. "I mean, really."

Jaguar sighed. No way out of this except right through the middle. "I think Daro's vision of Senci is accurate. Not that he's Dracula," she added hastily when she saw Clara's look, "But he's got psi capacities, some very powerful ones, and he's using them. We see that a lot on the Planetoids, so I recognize it when it comes up. That's what I know, and that's why I'm here. Senci's using psi capacities, and Daro needs an empath to protect him."

Clara frowned into her beer. "You're not saying Dr. Senci—he doesn't—" She paused, reconsidered her sentence. "He doesn't go around sucking blood or anything, right?"

"Well," Jaguar said, "maybe. I'm still not entirely sure."

Clara eyed her hard. Jaguar lifted a shoulder, let it drop. "There's some darker empathic practitioners who drink blood or use sex to access regenerative biochemicals. They prefer to get it from children, where it's still really fresh. I thought Senci was just your garden variety hypnopath, but apparently he's got some Telekine in him, too. The rest—it's not looking good."

Clara put her beer down hard. "I'll go for the psi capacity thing but if you think you can convince me—"

"Clara, you've got a warped disc, a missing transcript, and a brain-dead cop, not to mention my interview. You don't need to be convinced of anything. You just need help explaining what you already know. So you've come to the witch for a consult. At least," she added, grinning, "I don't charge."

Clara cleared her throat and poured some beer into herself. "I feel so weird about all this," she said. "I mean, I'm a regular sort of person. I don't even watch *Mysteries and History.*"

"I know," Jaguar sympathized. "But does it matter what Senci is as long as we get Daro through this? Once Senci's convicted he's on the Planetoid, and we aren't regular so it won't bother us."

"Okay," she said. "You're right. Eye on the Prize. So what'll Senci do next?"

Jaguar picked up her empty shot glass and held it to the light. Her instincts led her to places she wasn't sure Clara would follow, places she wasn't sure she was ready to go herself. She waved her glass at the bartender and got another.

"One thing we can count on," she said. "If there's already been one disc meltdown, we should assume Daro's voxchip is at risk."

"I got it locked up tight in the safe."

"And how'd that work last time? Does the safe have laser fencing? That interferes with psi capacities sometimes."

"Yeah. We don't always use it because it's a pain in the butt to turn on and off."

"You'll use it now. And I'll finish the interview with Senci tomorrow. See what I can get from him."

"You do that. Let me know how it goes." She lifted her beer and raised it to Jaguar. "And watch your back," she added. "Look out for runaway cabs."

Jaguar raised her tequila. "You, too."

* * * *

High on Jaguar's list of priorities when she left the bar was a shower, and a call to Alex. Someone she wouldn't have to explain the terms to. She walked down the street toward the hotel, the close heat comforting to her after the stale air of the artificially cooled bar. At least it was real, and she could feel it.

She stopped at a corner, waited for the traffic light to change. Overhead, wings buzzed. On the road, cars whizzed by. The night air had a softness, as of light diffused through mist. High humidity, and in the distance a rumbling of thunder. Across the street, a group of people stood waiting to go where she was now. They looked like sheep, she thought. A herd of sheep, all waiting for permission to move.

No. Not all of them.

A little girl pushed her way through a variety of legs and stepped onto the road, ready to dash out into traffic.

"No," Jaguar yelled, and ran out to grab her, stop her.

Cars slammed on brakes and laid on horns as Jaguar, unheeding, ran across the street.

The little girl stood still, her eyes huge with watching. She shook all over, as if she'd been hit with electric current, and then she turned around and ran away. Jaguar, ignoring the onlookers, went after her.

Wait, she said, reaching out to her. *I just want to talk. I don't want you to hurt yourself. I don't want to hurt you.*

The girl, almost half a block ahead, stopped running and turned to face her. Jaguar slowed her steps, not wanting to frighten her.

Who are you? she asked.

The little girl stared at her. *You ran into the cars. Why?*

I thought you'd hurt yourself. I wanted to help you.

She moved closer, and the little girl let her. She had to reach her, though. At least get close enough to know what she was. A ghost? Something from her own psyche? Her own past? What?

Help me? The girl questioned.

Help you. Jaguar confirmed. *Do you need help? Are you—safe?*

Almost there, moving slowly as if through thick water, taking her time. People passed her, passed the girl who watched with wide eyes.

Wide and wondering, as if Jaguar was something never seen before, something she couldn't quite understand.

My name is Maya, she whispered into Jaguar's thoughts.

Then, she turned and disappeared into the crowd.

CHAPTER 7

JAGUAR SAT IN THE GRAY ROOM, STARING at Dr. Senci's dense gray energy field. She could hardly see his face, except to know that a face was there. It smiled at her. At her back, she heard the hum of the camera, in all likelihood not recording the interaction.

She'd asked to have the laser fence turned off for this interview, thinking that might give her better access, but now she regretted it. Dr. Senci's presence made her breath go slow and thick, as if she breathed through sand. She caught the scent of something toxic in him.

Dr. Senci smiled and she felt him speaking into her mind, but she was better prepared for that today. She blocked it, quickly and thoroughly. No voice in her head today. She wouldn't allow it. His smile stayed, but grew tense at the edges.

"How is Daro?" he asked.

"He's well," Jaguar replied. "Why do you ask?"

"Being polite. Does he sleep?"

"Yes. He does now."

"And do you?"

Jaguar paused. No. She didn't sleep well. She was having dreams that woke her in a cold sweat. Dreams of choking. Dreams of Alex, bleeding from a wound made with her knife. Senci would see that. He would know that.

"Will you have children, Jaguar?" he asked.

An unexpected question, and not one she was ready to discuss. She remained quiet, keeping herself inside herself, as if she ducked to the bottom of a car sunk in deep water, sucking at the one pocket of air left, feeling the tons of cold water bearing down on her.

"Wouldn't you like to have children? A little girl of your own you can protect and teach the way your grandparents taught you. Or, maybe a little boy, like Daro. You're so alone. Without children, you'll grow old and die, alone."

She felt herself drifting down into his voice, seeing herself in the image he projected. She would be old, was growing older every day and her day would pass into endless night. She pushed it away, and was able to produce words.

"I've got a few years before I'm old," she said, and immediately felt better. The first words opened up the way for more. "And old isn't that bad."

"Not as bad as dead," Senci said.

She forced herself to laugh. "C'mon, Senci. You think your little psi tricks can work on me? If so, you don't know me at all. What is it you're doing anyway? Hypnopath stuff? Maybe a little telekinetic work mixed in?"

He sat attentively, his hands folded on his lap, his lips drawn tightly together. His voice spoke inside her, sliding beyond any blocking capacity she had.

You'd like that, wouldn't you Jaguar?

She pushed him away, spoke out loud. "I don't scare as easy as the children you bully and abuse. Only the truth works with me."

He sighed and reached across the table to her.

Give me your hand.

Jaguar watched her own hand lift and move to his. She asked it to return to her, but it wouldn't. As if he could command her body. As he held it, she saw the skin go white and cracked, the bones twisting. An illusion. Just a parlor trick. She could do that too. Any hypnopath could.

But the feeling that went with it was no hypnopath play. His touch stole from her. Stole energy, stole life.

"Dying isn't much fun, is it, Jaguar?" he asked, speaking out loud again.

She focused on her hand, asked it to become itself again, and it did. With effort, she pulled it away from him. "I wouldn't know. I haven't tried it yet."

Senci laughed softly. "You've come close, haven't you?"

His voice was thick inside her, a metal bar pressing into her brain.

You were a little girl when you stared down at your grandfather's body, still twitching, nerves not as ready to die as his heart, drained of blood by the bullets. The man who shot him lifted you and tossed you like a pillow onto the couch and held you down and pushed himself into you until you thought you would die, felt his death in you and looked into its eyes and said hello. Are you my death?

His eyes were dark like the wings of birds you dream about sometimes. They wanted to swallow you but they couldn't. Not entirely. He tried and failed and then he was gone and you never saw him again from that day to this. Remember, Jaguar?

The gray meat of old grief stuck in her teeth. Fishbones stabbed her throat, choking her. Her belly was filled with stones. When she breathed in, she tasted the air he expelled, and she couldn't stand it. He'd plucked this memory from her so easily, without her permission to enter ground she held sacred as a cemetery, her dead, dead past. Only a Telekine could do that, and so she was certain now about one more piece of the puzzle.

"I remember," she said out loud.

"But you're not afraid," he noted.

"No," she said.

He leaned closer and breathed in deeply, as if to drink this notion. Something important here, she thought, but she couldn't tell what.

Then, he leaned back and laughed. "You will be," he said, and he withdrew into himself.

The interview was over. Jaguar got up and left the room.

* * * *

When she left the building, she stood on the street corner outside for a good ten minutes, doing nothing except drinking in light. She was thirsty for light. Starved and parched for light. She let it flow into her, let it wash away what she'd inhaled down in the basement.

The streets were clean, and cheery people passed her, smiling and nodding politely. She wanted to say fuck you to them all.

Their smiles bothered her. They smiled as if they didn't know, wouldn't allow themselves to know what dirt they'd swept under their own rugs. Dr. Senci, under their feet, and they didn't even care. How many other killers from the Serials lived here, protected by their amnesty clause. She felt anger current through her, neurons and muscles, and let it drain out her hands. Let it go. Let it go.

She walked, not sure where she was going. Maybe back to the hotel. Maybe to get a drink. Maybe to go see Daro. Tomorrow was the first day of the trial, when the judges would review the list of witnesses and the first experts would testify about the voxchip. Daro didn't have to be there, but he asked if he could and his parents allowed it, under protest. She wanted to see him tonight, make sure he was okay before it started. But first she had to make sure she stood on solid ground.

She walked, aware of the sound of her own feet against the glittering pavement, aware of the electromag rumbling under her, aware of all the people who walked, unaware of resident evil, down the street with her.

The faces she saw were all strangers. She knew very few people on the home planet, and none of them lived in this city. She was lonely in a way she wasn't accustomed to, and at a bench outside a deli she stopped and sat, and did something she'd rarely done.

Her hand, opening and closing, sought a friend.

Alex, she called.

He was with her as quick as thought, and she knew he'd been waiting, open to her.

Here, Jaguar.

She didn't use words, didn't tell him about the interview with Dr. Senci. She just let him see the moment she was in now. Her presence in a city of strangers. Her concern for Daro. Her loneliness.

He returned a wordless comfort with the feel of a hand on her shoulder, a mouth briefly kissing her hair and a finger brushing her cheek. A courtly gesture from a man of profound courtesy.

Okay, Jaguar?

Yes. Okay. Okay now.

Planetoid Three—Toronto Replica, Zone 12

"How very odd," Alex muttered. He sat in his office, staring down at his hand, the sensation of her skin against it still tingling in his fingers.

She'd never contacted him for comfort. And she hadn't been specific about why she needed it, though she'd let a pretty heavy burden of sorrow run out of her. Then she was gone.

He wasn't sure if that was a good thing, or a bad thing. After some thought, he decided it was both. Good that she called to him. Bad that she was feeling this way. He'd call the hotel later, see if she was okay. According to his calendar, the trial started tomorrow. He hoped it would go speedily and well.

A quick knock on his door was followed by Rachel, poking her head in and saying, "Busy?"

"No more than usual. Come in."

She did, and slid a microdisc across his desk to him. "Pop that in and call up file S3," she said.

He did so, and noted that Rachel's face showed a very badly contained confusion. When the file scrolled across his screen, he viewed it.

"What am I looking at, Rachel?" he asked.

"I was going through Senci's file for previous offenses, thinking maybe I could pull something up for Jaguar to work with, right?"

"That's not really your job," Alex said.

"Sure. So as I was not really doing my job, I found out Senci has a previous record, kind of. At least, there's a DNA match for him on a child rape and murder charge."

Alex swiveled his whole body around to look at her. "There's nothing in the file—"

"I know. Look at the screen. You'll see why." Rachel pointed, and he looked.

Senci's DNA matched semen found in a seven year old girl murdered in Boston. But the name attached to the murder was James T. Smythe, never convicted because he disappeared before trial. The physical description was different than Senci, too. Smythe was blonde and stocky, older and shorter. But the DNA was a match.

"Where did you get this?" he asked.

Rachel shifted from one foot to another. "It's kind of weird, really. I was running Senci's DNA through a global check—just poking around, you know? It pulled up a lab experiment on cold cases, using old evidence to see how long it held up over time. This murder was part of it. The girl's dress had semen on it, so they tested it and put the results in their system. It came up as a match with Senci. But see—it's old."

Alex felt something cold enter the room, take a seat, and have a laugh at his expense. "How old?" he asked.

"About 200 years. At the time, Smythe was 51."

Alex was silent. Dr. Senci's DNA was on a crime committed 200 years ago.

"Weird, isn't it?" Rachel asked.

"I'm afraid it may make more sense than I'd like it to," Alex replied.

CHAPTER 8

Home Planet—Toronto, Canada

THE PRIMARY JUDGE, HONORABLE REX BANNUR, M.D., SPOKE FIRST.

"Our task today," he said, "is to determine whether the recorded evidence against Dr. Senci is admissible. We'll begin with expert testimony for the prosecution, and then hear from the defense."

The transcriber spoke into his bell-like apparatus and his words were entered into a computer log as he spoke. The other two judges—panelists they were called, as if it was a game show, Jaguar thought—listened solemnly, but without much excitement.

The primary judge, Dr. Bannur, would be responsible for all matters of protocol. The others, The Honorable Doctors Katherine Delorn, and Daniel Serino, would continue to listen solemnly and without much excitement, perhaps asking questions now and then. Daro and his parents, Clara and her assistant Gary, and Jaguar were on one side of the courtroom. On the other side there was only Dr. Senci and his lawyer. Behind them, the expert witnesses for prosecution and defense. No spectators allowed. All drama forbidden.

Jaguar was used to procedural meetings. She'd attended enough exit meetings for prisoners to understand the nature of legal ritual which was, for the most part, stultifyingly dull. Nobody expected any surprises today, not from the expert witnesses for Daro's side or Dr. Senci's. Later, after the decision to admit or not admit the voxchip, after the judges listened to it, they might not need any other witnesses. If they did, they had two doctors who would testify that Daro wasn't delusional, a teacher to testify for his honesty in school, and Daro's recorded interview, done in the presence of both defense and prosecuting attorney.

Dr. Senci's witnesses besides the voxchip expert would be parents of other children he had helped, a medical colleague who would testify about other cases Dr. Senci had worked on with him. Then Dr. Senci would testify, and it would be over.

But for today, it was all about the voxchip and whether or not it had been tampered with.

Daro was already nervous. He squirmed, sandwiched between his parents and Jaguar, trying to be quiet but unable to be still. Jaguar didn't blame him. She wished she was young enough to squirm.

As the expert for the prosecution took his oath and started answering questions she tried to listen, but found herself tuning out pretty quickly. She'd stayed late with Daro last night, playing VR games with him before she went back to her hotel and collapsed into a series of bad dreams. In the morning she found a message from Alex, but she hadn't had time to return it yet. Better to speak with him after they went through this morning's proceedings, which were too predictable to hold her restless attention.

Regarding the recording Daro had made, their expert said all his tests came up clean, and besides, it was ludicrous to think a twelve-year-old boy could tamper with a voxchip at that level of sophistication. He talked about wave sine correlations, damage warps, overlap sequences, used other technobabble Jaguar could almost decipher. The defense lawyer cross-examined him to no avail. He wouldn't budge. Then he was done.

When he left the stand, the panelists turned to Dr. Senci's lawyer. "Your witness may be called now," Dr. Bannur said.

The lawyer at Senci's side stood, cleared his throat. "Your honor," he said, "we won't be calling an expert to speak to this issue."

The Judges whispered among themselves and then the Honorable Katherine DeLorn asked the obvious question. "What's the reason for this change?"

The lawyer cleared his throat again. "It was my client's decision."

Clara looked to Jaguar, her eyes asking the question, 'what the hell?'

Jaguar had no answer. She'd filled Clara in on her interview with Senci, which hadn't recorded, and told her she now knew the guy was a hypnopath and a telekine and explained those terms.

And now this. Senci wasn't calling an expert witness to say the voxchip was false. She didn't like the implications at all.

The judges concluded their consultation. "We'll convene to consider our decision regarding the admissibility of Prosecution's evidence."

They rose. Everyone else rose. They left. Everyone else sat back down.

"I'm staying," Clara said to Jaguar. "My guess is they'll be back real soon."

And she was right.

They re-entered the room in less than ten minutes, let everyone present rise and be seated again, then Dr. Bannur fixed a pallid eye on the people in the courtroom.

"We have determined the voxchip labeled exhibit A is admissible to these proceedings as evidence in the case of Karas vs. Senci. Let it be duly noted."

His gavel came up. His gavel went down. Jaguar saw Clara's shoulders drop, as if she'd been holding them about half an inch higher than usual throughout. Daro scribbled furiously on a piece of paper. Jaguar took it from him, read, then passed it on to Clara.

"What does that mean?" he had written.

"It means we're on second base," Clara wrote back.

Daro read her response and nodded solemnly.

"We'll take a forty-five minute recess to review the voxchip," Judge Bannur concluded. They rose again and left the room.

Clara nodded at Daro and his parents. "It's a good time for you guys to go get a soda," she said. She ruffled Daro's hair. "Go play some VR tennis. There's a machine in the cafeteria. We'll call you back in when it's time."

"Get some coffee?" Clara asked Jaguar when Daro left.

Jaguar looked around. Dr. Senci was speaking in low tones with his lawyer. The transcriber had followed the panelists out of the room.

"I'll stick," she said.

Clara followed the direction of Jaguar's eyes, to Dr. Senci. "Suit yourself," she said. "But don't do anything stupid."

"Never," Jaguar said, biting back a grin as she thought of what Alex would say to that.

Clara left, and she relaxed back into her seat. She'd stay and keep an eye on Dr. Senci. His decision not to call their expert witness, the way he made it public, had the feel of a threat or a challenge.

She folded into herself and breathed deeply, seeking the energy she could surround him with to hold him still, keep him from doing harm. Just a shield, without direct contact. That should be enough.

It was quiet here, and dark.

Dark, and unexpectedly cold.

Not cold like winter air moving in, but cold like heat drained away. A hollow coldness, like a scar cupped in flesh. She was drawn into this hollow as if she would fill the vacuum that nature abhors. As if that was her job.

She was being pulled. She glanced over at Senci and saw he was smiling. Smiling at her.

A fine trembling ran across her body, uncontrollable and without discernible origin. She wasn't afraid. She wasn't afraid. She looked down at her hands and saw they weren't trembling.

Look again, Jaguar, a voice said.

She blinked, and saw that her hands rested on a dress which was grey and red checkered. An old dress. A dress from her childhood.

Remember, Jaguar? Look again.

The dress became her suit again, but now a small circular metal chip rested in her hand. A voxchip. The metal shimmered, dissolved into liquid and held its shape for a brief moment before running through her fingers. She tried to catch it as it oozed away but it was gone. Simply gone.

"No," she whispered. "No."

The room shifted. The cold dispersed. She looked to Dr. Senci and saw that he no longer smiled at her. Instead, he was reading the newspaper, calm and composed.

The door at the back of the courtroom opened and people came in. Clara, bailiffs and lawyers entered the space.

"All rise," a bailiff said, and they did.

"Jaguar, you okay?" Clara whispered in her ear.

"Where's Daro?" she whispered back.

"Still at lunch. I thought it'd take longer. I didn't have time to get them. You sure you're okay?"

Jaguar shook herself. "I'll let you know after the judges talk," she said.

* * * *

They talked, but none of what they said was good.

Something about the voxchip. Something about it being damaged. Unusable.

"Nothing on it at all," Dr. Bannur remonstrated. "Of course, we understand that technical failures occur, but it was the responsibility of your office to bring us clean evidence."

"Your honor," Clara said, "it was in perfect condition when we gave it to you. Our expert witness testified to that. I haven't any idea what's happened, but we have a notarized transcript of the recording, and since I've heard it, and the expert witness heard it, I suggest we admit the transcript as evidence and call one of us as verifying witnesses."

The judges weren't so sure. They consulted with their protocol bailiff, who said no, the transcripts weren't admissible without the original source intact.

Jaguar turned toward Dr. Senci, glaring at him.

She became aware of a break in the proceedings. The judges whispered among themselves, reminding Jaguar of the witches in Macbeth. One of them pointed. Pointed toward her. They called the bailiff to them, whispered to him.

He turned and faced the courtroom, cleared his throat and spoke. "The Judges request that the woman in the blue suit make her face less expressive. It disturbs them."

She looked to her right and her left, then at her blue suit. She pointed at herself.

"Me?" she mouthed. The bailiff nodded. She frowned and looked toward Dr. Senci, who sat with his eyes closed, considering the nothing behind his eyelids.

The judges continued to talk and talk and talk.

* * * *

They finally decided to proceed if the prosecution was willing to let Daro answer questions after his recorded interview was viewed. Now, he'd also have to answer to the defense, and Senci would be in the room while he did so.

After this pronouncement, they called another recess. Clara grabbed Jaguar's arm and led her toward the waiting room. "Jesus," she said, "I wish I knew what the hell was happening here. You got any clue, I'd appreciate it."

Jaguar, still feeling dazed, shook her head. "Clara, what does this mean for the case?"

"Nothing good," she said. "Now we got Daro, in the presence of the monster man. *Punto*. Nothing else. It all rests on him."

"Where is he?" Jaguar asked.

"At a deli down the street."

"Listen, you go get him. I need to report in."

"Okay. Don't be too long, though. Daro'll want you here."

"I know," Jaguar said.

* * * *

She found a telecom in an empty office, and punched in Alex's code, cueing his personal line so he'd pick up rather than let the switchboard field it for him. When his face appeared, she felt unexpected relief.

He started a smile, then studied her face. "What's wrong?" he asked.

"The voxchip failed," she told him. "No copies allowed, and no testimony as to its contents."

"What?"

"The voxchip. Daro's evidence. It played nothing. The lawyer listened to it before she handed it in and it was fine. The judges insist there's no way anyone could tamper with it, so they blame the prosecution—for giving them sullied evidence is how they put it. And Alex—there's more."

"Tell me," he said. "Not on the lines. Just—tell me."

She breathed in and focused, found him waiting and receptive. She gave him all that had happened so far. The little girl, Maya, still following her. How Clara had told her about the earlier interview, the other voxchip failure, the dying cop. Then her own interview with Senci, how he made her hand grow old, what it felt like to be in the room with him with his toxic breath and his fetid energy field and his coldness. When she was through, she left him easily as a sigh.

He rubbed at the back of his ear. Material dispersal was a Telekine skill, and the hand trick belonged to the hypnopath, But the rest. The grey energy field and toxic breath, along with what Rachel brought him yesterday. There really wasn't any doubt left. All he had to do now was confirm what she already knew.

"There's something Rachel found out," he said. "About Senci. He has a record."

He told her and she grew quiet. Calm. All shields up and running. All information going through the mill of possibilities. Even Protean changers couldn't create exact DNA matches. And why would Senci shift his DNA to match a child-killer? The evidence led to only one possible explanation. They'd caught a mythic creature. A Greenkeeper.

Jaguar's response was typical of her. "We have to keep Daro safe," she said. "And we have to stop this monster."

Alex nodded. That was the right order. Keep the boy safe, then stop the monster. If they could. "Can you block him?" he asked.

"He's strong, Alex. The energy drain—I haven't dealt with that before."

"Nasty," he agreed, feeling what she'd shown him from the interview. "Any residual damage?"

"Fatigue. Depression. It passes."

She clenched and unclenched her jaw, her gaze moving restlessly around the room as if she expected attack. For the first time since he'd known her, Alex read fear of failure in her, a sense that she was facing more than she could handle. He saw her deliberately shake it off, bring it under control. She would not admit it to her presence.

"Blocking's probably pointless," she said. "It makes more sense to go on the offensive. If I could get into him, I might understand him better. Figure out his agenda."

"No," Alex said firmly. "That's his hook. Don't bite it. Don't let fear dictate your moves."

"I'm not afraid of him," she said stubbornly.

"But you're afraid of something," he returned. "That's no way to go on the offensive. And you should be afraid, Jaguar. What he can do, how long he's been doing it for—neither of us have ever dealt with anything like it."

"We have to do something," she insisted. "He's got a plan, and I need to know what it is."

That gave him pause. "What do you mean, a plan?"

"Alex, he got caught," she said, emphasizing each word. "Greenkeepers don't get caught unless they want to. So why did he?"

He found his heart was pounding harder than it should be. He reached for Adept space, seeking an answer, and found only darkness. Only cold.

"I'm thinking," he said out loud, "maybe you should get off the case. Take a shuttle back here later today."

"I can't leave Daro alone with a monster," she said.

"Who said you would? I'll take over for you," he said.

"A man abused him. He wouldn't trust you, especially not now. If I go, he's alone."

She was right. He didn't like it, but he couldn't deny it. "Then I'll join you there."

"No. I need you clear of this. A clear voice, in case I get unclear."

Okay, he thought. So at least she recognized that she wasn't omnipotent. That was also new and disconcerting. He drummed his fingers on his desk.

"Listen," he said, "focus on Daro and don't engage with Senci. Not yet. You understand? He'll try to pull you in, but don't go there. Nobody's better at closing off than you are, so stay as closed as possible, and keep a good physical distance from him. It sounds like he can't do as much when he's further away. Just deal with the boy, the court stuff. We'll figure out what to do with Senci once Daro is out of it. You got that?"

"I got it," she said crisply, though her face was grim.

"Good. How about his law guardian? Is she up to speed on any of this?"

"As much as she can absorb. She's on my side—and definitely on Daro's."

"Are any of the judges likely to be sympathetic?"

"Not them. They're fish-heads. Board of Sturgeons. They asked me to make my face less expressive because it disturbs them."

Alex grinned. "Maybe I should tell them what it does to me." He was glad to see her bite back on a smile.

"You don't take a minute off, do you?" she asked.

"Not when I'm courting. It's full-time work. Have you talked to Jake and One Bird?"

She shook her head. "Not yet. I will."

"Right away. As soon as we're done. If anyone can help, they can." He cast around for anything else he could do. The only other option he could see was kidnapping her. She certainly wouldn't leave of her own volition, and he understood why. "How's the boy holding up?" he asked.

"Okay so far. He'll be there when they roll his video testimony. He has to go through questioning, with the voxchip gone."

"Brave kid."

"A good kid. I wish I felt more assured about the outcome."

"I'll call in some favors and get extra patrols down there for him. And the lawyer. She might be in danger, too." And you, he thought. Not that she'd worry about that. "Jaguar, don't underestimate what we're facing," he said. "Take care. Take a good deal of care."

"I will, but care doesn't seem to help much around here. I hope I'm wrong."

Alex nodded. So did he.

* * * *

When Alex's face disappeared, Jaguar punched in the number for Jake and One Bird's house. After two rings, One Bird's smiling visage appeared in the viewscreen. She turned and called, "Jake? C'mere. It's Jaguar."

She heard him approach and when his angular features appeared behind One Bird's soft and broad face he was frowning. He didn't like telecoms. He said all that machinery got in the way.

"It's good to see you," Jaguar said. "How are you?"

"Good," One Bird said.

"Old," Jake chimed in.

Jaguar smiled. "Better than dead."

Jake sniffed. "When you try it, you can tell me. You got trouble."

A statement rather than a question. Jaguar didn't ask how he knew. He always knew. She nodded. "I'm dealing with something big, and I have to protect someone. A little boy. He's got a monster by the tail." She used a Mertec word that meant pure evil, and was the equivalent of vampire in that language.

"Tell us," One Bird said. Jaguar did, speaking subvocally. When she was done, Jake rubbed at his balding head and One Bird chewed her lip. They looked at each other. Jake said something in his native Zuni. One Bird replied in her own Tzutijil Maya. They often carried on long conversations that way, much to the confusion of anyone who tried to follow. This talk was brief, and simple enough that Jaguar understood.

This is it, Jake had said. It looks that way, One Bird had replied.

Before she could ask what they meant, they turned back to her and One Bird spoke.

"Your boundaries are weak," she said. "Work with them. You remember how we taught you?"

"Yes. Of course," she said. "Anything else?"

"You have to come here," One Bird said.

"I can't," Jaguar said. "I have to take care of the boy."

"Not yet," Jake said. "When it's over. Then you come here."

One Bird nodded. "You come here to us when it's over. You agree?"

To agree was to be honor bound, but she gladly assented. The thought of the clean air and the clear sky there sounded like her idea of heaven right now. "What do I do now?" she asked. "How do I protect Daro?"

One Bird and Jake exchanged glances. "Stay close to him," One Bird said. "He'll need you to—to help him let go. You know how." She used a word that meant releasing a spirit from bondage, used for possession or at the point of death. It was a specific energy, a specific prayer and cleansing. She hadn't done it in a while. And if they were advising it, she'd probably need it.

"Go over it with me," she said.

"Like this," Jake said, and showed her the feel of it, reminded her of the words used and why they were used. When he was done he waited.

She took a moment to absorb it, make it her own. "Okay," she said. "I got it."

"Yeah, you do. And stay clear of the monster," Jake added. "Don't try anything with him."

Just what Alex said. She supposed they were right. They usually were. "I'll have to deal with him sooner or later. There must be some way I can—"

"No," Jake cut in. "Just stay with the boy. Don't leave him. And when it's over, come here."

Jaguar let the words settle in, took another moment to formulate her thoughts, then spoke. "I don't know if I can stay clear," she said. "He—he pulls me."

They watched her in silence for a moment, feeling this. Jake passed a hand over his face and swore softly.

"Stop listening to him," he said. "You believe what he says. It's a lie."

"It feels… true," she said. "As if there's something…."

Jake started to speak, but One Bird put a hand on his arm. "There is something," she said softly, "But not what you think, and not what he says. We'll straighten it out when you get here. Right now, any attention you give him makes him stronger. Don't *feed* him. Just be with the boy until it's over."

Jake grunted an agreement, and they were silent.

"Is that it?" Jaguar asked.

Jake looked up, considering. "You could try the earth walk prayer," he said.

"Would it do any good?"

"Probably not. But you could try it."

"What did you mean," she asked, "When you said this is it?"

Jake tilted his head at her. "Did I teach you Zuni?"

"No. But I learned a little. And some Tzutijil. So what did you mean? Have you been expecting this?"

"Yes," One Bird said directly. "This, or something like it."

She didn't ask how or why they knew. Probably they'd seen it in a sweat lodge ceremony or a dream. She wasn't surprised. There were some big energies floating around this one, and they'd feel it.

"You through, or you got something else to complain about?" Jake asked.

She tried a grin, and it almost worked. "Not a thing. So what's happening there?"

"The usual. Maria Tekas needs a sweat so we'll be doing that tonight. Jimmy'll stay here. You remember Jimmy?"

"I remember," Jaguar said. He was one of many young men One Bird had done her best to get Jaguar to marry, before she'd gone to the Planetoids to work.

"He's not married yet," One Bird said. "Believe it?"

"Guess he hasn't found the right woman."

"Or he found her and couldn't hold onto her. You can see him when you come."

"Sure," Jaguar said. "Listen, thanks for the advice."

One Bird reached a hand out and touched the screen as if she was touching Jaguar's face. "Remember who you are," she said. "Stay near the boy."

"We'll do what we can from here," Jake added. "And we'll see you soon."

Without goodbye, they disappeared from the screen. They never said goodbye to her. They had no word for it.

* * * *

The return of the Judges was a letdown in tension. They ordered a recess until the morning, when they'd watch Daro's taped interview and have him answer follow-up questions in the presence of Dr. Senci and his lawyer. If the lawyer had questions after that, he could ask them. Philip and Susan seemed confused by the whole sequence of events, and after a brief conference with Clara, Philip pulled Jaguar aside.

"The prosecution's fallen on its face, hasn't it?" he asked her in a low voice.

"No," she said. "The voxchip was destroyed. We don't know how it happened, but it's not Clara's fault."

He wasn't convinced. "I wish I'd hired a private attorney. Didn't seem necessary at the time, but now...."

"There's nothing anyone could do. Just take Daro home and see that he gets some rest."

Daro, hearing his name, turned from Clara, who was giving him a pep talk, toward Jaguar. "You'll come over tonight?" he asked.

"Of course," she said. "Just lemme get out of this stupid suit, and we can have a catch."

Clara nodded at her. Good idea, her eyes said. Be there with him. Be there for him.

So she went back to her hotel, changed her clothes and went back to the Karas house. Susan told her Daro was out back, in his woodshed. Daro said she could find him there. Jaguar read resentment at this permission, not given lightly. But she wasn't here for the parents. She was here for Daro.

She walked across the yard to the small shed and knocked on the door. He mumbled something, and she went inside. He was sitting on a high stool at a worktable, a piece of smooth wood growing smoother under his hands. Curled shavings cluttered the floor and the space carried their clean, sharp scent.

She closed the door. The shed walls were plastered with posters of his favorite musicians—Tamo Boruni and the Blasters. He'd told her about them. The Blasters sang about real stuff, he said. War and fear and the dark man who came in the night for you.

He looked up at her, his face pale and tired.

"Me again," she said. "How're you doing?"

"How do you think?" he asked, scowling. He saw her wince in response, and was glad of it. There. Some of his pain gone. Then he blushed, ashamed of himself, though he didn't know why. Every time he turned around he felt ashamed of himself. Every question another lawyer or shrink asked him he felt ashamed. Sometimes he was sorry he ever told.

"I brought you some mint," Jaguar said. "It helps keep your mind clear."

She held out a thick bunch, dried and wrapped. He eyed her suspiciously, then took it from her, held it up to his nose and breathed in deeply.

"That's what you smell like," he noted.

He toyed with the bundle, put it on the worktable next to him. "Thanks," he said, then went back to his task, smoothing wood. Smoothing it, soothing himself.

Jaguar leaned against his workbench and watched. His hands moved without breaks in motion. She pointed at the tool he was using. "What's that?" she asked.

"An adze. Don't you know an adze when you see one?"

"I do now. Old tool, isn't it? Aren't there electronic versions?"

"Yeah. I tried one once. They're noisy. Feel this," he said, reaching over and taking her hand in his, bringing it over to the curving piece he was working at. He pressed her hand against the wood and rubbed it back and forth. It was silky and clean.

"Nice," she said. "Like glass."

He nodded, and released her hand. That was the first time he'd ever touched her. She brought her hand up to her face and breathed in the scent of wood.

"Is it mahogany?" she asked.

"That's right," he said. "You can tell by the smell?"

She nodded. "It's an art I know. Tree identification."

He narrowed his eyes at her. "You *are* an empath, aren't you?"

That was unexpected. "I am," she admitted, "Does that frighten you?"

He shrugged. "No. But this book I read, it said empaths know things by smell. Is that true?"

Jaguar couldn't help but laugh. She knew the book he meant. It was a religious polemic against the evils of the empathic arts. It said that empaths were low as dogs and like dogs they knew things through their sense of smell.

"Not unless we practice that way of knowing things," she said. "We do know things without words, though. In the same way a cat or dog will know something without words, by the energy they sense."

He considered this. "The mint—that's an empath thing?"

"Yes," she said. "I use it when I'm dealing with prisoners. To stay safe from their shadow."

"It's to keep me safe from him, isn't it?"

She nodded.

He sighed. "Are you gonna read my mind?" he asked.

"Not unless you want me to," she said. "Empaths actually do something a little different, anyway. We like to know how people are feeling and what they experience. Not just what they're thinking. "

He twisted his face around. "He's a vampire, y'know," was his next comment. "Everyone thinks that's like some fantasy I have. Like my nightmares. But it's not. It's real."

Beating in his veins, she heard it again. Didn't have to listen hard because it was all over him.

I won't become him won't let myself become what he is

"I know what he is," Jaguar said, keeping her voice even.

He didn't look at her, but his hand stopped in its motion. "You believe me," he said.

"I don't have to," she said. "I know it for myself."

"I don't want to become one."

"You won't. I won't let it happen."

His hand stopped, lay still against the wood. "You can help me?" he whispered.

"I can. Let's get through the trial, then I'll explain it to you."

Relief shuddered through him, from his shoulders down. "Okay," he said.

"Put some music on. I haven't heard any good music since I left the Planetoid."

She found herself an old box to sit on and relaxed, letting the afternoon waste itself around them. He would testify tomorrow, and before then, they needed whatever peace of mind they could grab.

CHAPTER 9

THE TAPED INTERVIEW ROLLED, and all eyes stayed on it. Daro spoke carefully, calmly, about his sessions with Dr. Senci. How the sexual interaction began, with Dr. Senci telling him it was a way to relax, and relaxing would make the nightmares go away. Daro said he recorded a session because he didn't think it was right and he wanted to tell his mother, but it was hard to talk about that kind of stuff to someone like your mother. Just giving her the voxchip would be easier. She always asked what they did in sessions, anyway.

The lawyer asked how he made the tape, and he explained about his earchip, and how he'd reversed the panel to get it to record. His face grew animated as he explained, but clouded over when he was asked about his nightmares. He said quietly, "I had nightmares about vampires."

And did he think Dr. Senci was a vampire, the lawyer asked.

Daro shrugged. "I don't know what he is, but I don't like him."

A good close.

The judges finished the notes they were making and then requested Daro's presence at the bench. He walked up, took his oath, took a seat.

Dr. Bannur cleared his throat. "Daro," he said, "how old are you?"

"Twelve last month."

"I see. Now what do you suppose happened to the recording you made?"

"I don't know. Maybe somebody did something to it."

"Do you think so?"

Daro turned back and looked at his law guardian, who had to keep herself from leading him in any way. "Just answer the question, Daro," she said.

"Don't work this too hard, Daro," Jaguar said quietly to herself. She reached out to him, making light empathic contact, just enough to send some reassurance.

As soon as she did, it hit her.

Like a wave—a shock wave of sound pouring through her, a voice booming in her head.

You are mine I made you mine you can't escape. You are mine. You are mine. You are mine.

She brought a hand up to her head. Dr. Senci, speaking in Daro. He'd gotten in—how? Because she made contact? She immediately closed and looked to the judges, who were waiting for Daro to speak. Clara, whose eyes were on the judges. Daro's parents who sat carefully composed, a still life.

But Daro couldn't speak. He was choking, trying for words but his eyes were wide from pressure inside his skull. His voice spiraled into a high-pitched whine.

Won't become him won't let him become me can't help me help me help me.

She had to do something. She held a hand up and out toward him, palm out, and focused her energy.

Daro, let go. Easy. I'll protect you.

But he couldn't hear her. Not anymore. Senci had him.

Stay with the boy, One Bird said. Stay clear of Senci, they all said. But she couldn't do both. To contact Daro was to find Senci. To find Senci was to be trapped. And since she couldn't make it better, she'd take her fall-back position and make it worse.

She turned her awareness away from Daro, directed it all to Dr. Senci. She'd distract him, take him out of Daro's mind and into hers. He was across the aisle, across the room, and near enough to laugh down the back of her neck. She felt his attention move to her. Daro's choking words subsided into coughing.

The judges fretted. "Is he ill?" One of them asked.

Clara stood. "Could he have a glass of water?"

A judge nodded, and the bailiff brought one over to him. Daro lifted it, took a sip.

Jaguar kept her awareness around Dr. Senci, surrounding him with it. Standing between him and the boy. She felt him push against her, and she didn't move. He was testing her.

Go ahead. Hit me with your best shot, buddy.

Anything, as long as he stayed away from Daro, who could speak again, his voice a low murmur just outside her hearing. She had to stay focused on Senci so Daro could go on. She felt the push again, stood firm against it, and then felt a withdrawal.

Dr. Senci stopped pushing, and began to pull instead.

He was pulling her. Pulling her away from herself, draining her as if he'd pulled a plug. As if he knew how to breathe the chromosomes out of her, her soul just water flowing into him, into that empty space he seemed to be.

You are bound to me. Bound to me. See what happens to them if you try to escape.

Drained of energy, she couldn't hold her ground and the connection was severed. She looked to Daro, who began to writhe in pain. His voice became a wailing cry, wild and weird in this sterile room.

"He—he's a vampire," Daro keened, voice high as wind on a mountain. "He makes people do things. I don't want to become him I won't become him make him stop make him stop."

make him stop make him stop make him stop.

Jaguar was up and out of her seat. Clara got there first, and between the two of them they lifted him from his seat and moved him out of the courtroom. His parents, white with shock, were close behind. The judges mumbled to each other and a recess was called for the rest of the day.

* * * *

Jaguar stayed with Daro until he fell asleep, then dragged herself back to her hotel and called Clara, who was reassuring.

"It's not a disaster," she said. "Maybe just the opposite. The judges felt sorry for Daro. They gave Senci the fish eye, like, you did this to him you nasty man. You never know with judges. They can tilt either way with something like this. Besides, Senci's got to testify tomorrow. He's an arrogant son of a bitch, and I know how to hang them."

"I'll bet you do," Jaguar said. Then, "Clara, I want you to stay in my room tonight."

Clara laughed. "Listen, you're a pretty woman and all, but I'm not wired that way."

"Dammit, I'm not joking. I want to keep an eye on you."

As if, she thought, that made any difference. She couldn't protect Daro and he was in the room with her. Still, she valued the illusion of control. Needed it desperately tonight.

"You mean that, don't you?"

"People drop dead around this case," Jaguar said. "Equipment fails. Evidence dissipates itself. If that's about to happen to you, I want to watch. So if you won't come here, I'll park my ass on your doorstep. Got a preference?"

Clara laughed. "Okay. Tell you what. I'll pack up my stuff and you meet me here. There's a great Indian restaurant around the corner. We'll treat ourselves like real people, then go back to your hotel and get drunk."

"See you in twenty," Jaguar said.

Once she was dressed she opted for a cab, which dropped her at a U-shaped apartment building that stood with its concave side facing another building exactly like it. In between the two was a courtyard with gardens and cobblestone walks, a fountain, benches, tables with umbrellas all around it. There was a replica of these buildings on the Planetoid, not too far from the Teacher's offices. It almost made her feel at home.

She walked to the front entrance. Clara was supposed to be waiting for her. A security guard sat just inside the front door, staring at her. She didn't want to hang around making him nervous so she made a motion as if she was pulling out a swipe card to get in.

He nodded, watched her. She moved her hand over the swipe patch, hoping it would give. She had a gift for mucking with technology, and was particularly good with a lock. She used to let herself in to Alex's building that way, before he relented and gave her a key.

The door opened. She waved as she strolled past the guard, took the elevator up to the 12th floor. She was about to knock on Clara's door when she heard laughter that twisted into a booming sound. Large, and hollow and cold, it rolled through her like thunder.

She waited for it to subside. Waited more for what might happen next. Nothing did.

She put her hand on Clara's door and slipped the lock, walked inside and stood there, feeling emptiness.

"Clara?" she asked. Nobody answered.

The living room window was open and she went to it, but she didn't look down. Not yet.

"Clara?" she asked again. More silence. No, she thought. No. This is not acceptable. "Clara, where the fuck are you?" she shouted.

She could hear water bubbling in the fountain twelve stories down. She looked out the window, and down.

Down to the rose bushes in the courtyard, bursting with red blooms.

Down to the cobblestones, and the flower of a woman's body, pouring red over the ground.

Clara's body, broken on the stones.

"Clara," she whispered. "Clara."

* * * *

Jaguar spent the rest of the night answering questions. The police. The Provincial Attorney's office. More police. Forms and statements and reports. She drank too much coffee and it made her veins buzz with adrenalin. She had to ID the body before it went to the morgue, then sit at Clara's table and answer more questions and more.

After she'd told her story for the tenth time she eyed the cops coldly. "Look," she said, "Arrest me, or let me go. And while you're making up your minds, get me a telecom. I want to call my Supervisor on Planetoid 3 and report this."

A homicide detective pulled the cops away from her. Someone put a telecom on the table next to her. She stared at it, calculated what time it would be where Alex was. He'd be at home. Or not at home. But he wouldn't be at his office.

She punched in his code and listened to his message tell her he wasn't home. When it was done she said, "Neither am I. Do me a favor. When you get home call this number." She gave Clara's telecom code. "A homicide cop will answer. His name's Harrison. Explain to him what I'm doing here and why, in all likelihood, I'm not a murderer. Ta ta."

She pushed the telecom away. An officer came over and stood near her while a multitude of officials invaded the remnants of Clara's privacy. Forensics, crime scene specialists, cops and more cops. Harrison slapped a piece of paper on the table.

"What do you make of that?" he asked.

She considered a variety of rude responses and discarded them. She looked at the paper, but he wouldn't let her touch it.

It was an old take-out menu, written over in red lipstick.

THIS CASE IS FUCKED WAS FROM THE START I WON'T BECOME HIM TELL JAGUAR SHE KNOWS NO TIME

And the name. Clara.

She stared blankly up at the officer. "Where'd you find it?" she asked.

"In the bathroom. Stuffed behind the toilet."

Jaguar felt sinking sorrow. Clara. The last moments of her life spent scratching out messages in lipstick, hiding in a bathroom. Jaguar, moving her hand closer to the paper, could feel the terror of it, the shock of approaching death, the attempt to drive it away.

"Now what do you suppose she meant?" Harrison asked.

Jaguar lowered her face into her hands. She wouldn't shed tears in front of this man.

"She says tell Jaguar. Says Jaguar knows. So what do you know?" Harrison demanded

"Not a fucking thing," she said through her hands. "If I did, Clara wouldn't be dead."

"Yeah," the officer said, "Right."

Jaguar crossed her arms on the table and lowered her head. Harrison called out, "Hey, Joe. Make some more coffee. The lady's tired, and it looks like we're gonna be here for awhile."

* * * *

He was right. They kept her there for hours, until the telecom buzzed and Harrison took it out of the room. When he returned, he handed it to Jaguar, and she saw Alex's face, looking ominous.

"I'm pulling you off the assignment, Dr. Addams," he said. "I want you back here on the next shuttle."

She resisted the urge to curse like a sailor. Instead, she stayed formal. "That would be an egregious error, Supervisor," she said, speaking crisply. Nothing sounded better to her than leaving this city, this country, this planet, but she couldn't. He knew that. "The job's not done. I stay until the trial's over. It's protocol."

"Protocol be damned. You're not even close to safe and you can't stay there."

"I have to. Your emotions are clouding your judgment."

He glowered at her. "Dr. Addams, I have never—"

"—Never slept with one of your Teachers before," she cut in. Behind her, Harrison coughed loudly. She turned and showed him a grin.

Alex was silent. The shot hit home. She went subvocal.

If you want to court me, you have to court who I am, not what you're afraid will happen to me.

He pulled himself away, glowered some more, then smoothed his face.

"Okay," he said. "You're right. I apologize."

She felt her shoulders relax. Off one cliff, and on to the next. "Can you get these cops off my back?" she asked.

"Already done. I had a talk with them." He went subvocal again.

Can they get Senci for Clara?

Not a chance. He's wired until the trial's over. The perfect alibi.

He offered a few appropriate responses, then returned to speaking out loud. "What's next for you?"

"Back to my hotel. Tomorrow—or I guess it's already today—see what the legal team says. I haven't got a clue how they'll handle it."

"I'm having some of these gentlemen park their asses outside your room until the trial's over."

"Alex, it won't—

"—It might. And I'll be watching, too. All night long. In the meantime, don't try anything on your own. If it becomes necessary to take," he paused, searching for a word, "to take unusual action, get in touch with me first. You don't go this alone, is that clear?"

"Abundantly," she said.

"Good. Get through this with Daro, then haul ass back here. We'll figure something out."

"Alex, listen," she said. "I don't think I'm in danger—at least, not the same kind Clara was. I think—I think he wants me alive."

Alex shuddered. That was probably the most horrid piece of good news he'd ever heard. He eyed her. "What makes you think that?"

"You know," she said, and raised a hand in the gesture of the empath. She had clear-seeing as one of her arts. She'd sensed this.

"All the more reason to stay away from him. And do me a favor. Remember how—how precious you are. In my absence, treat yourself that way."

Before she could respond, he nodded once, and was gone. But already she sensed his watching, like hands shielding an injured bird from harm. She sighed. He couldn't keep that up forever, but she was glad of it for now.

Jaguar looked up at Harrison, who was torn between juicy interest and bewilderment. She pressed her hands on the table and stood. On her way out she patted him on the shoulder. He seemed to need it.

* * * *

When she got back to her hotel and laid her body down, she found it could no longer remember the sleep command. She tossed her way through a few hours of fitful half-dreams, then got out of bed and spent the early morning with Daro and his family, trying to offer them reassurances she didn't have. While she was with them, they got a call from the Prosecution's office telling them the last day of testimony was postponed until tomorrow.

Jaguar got on the phone for particulars and learned the assistant prosecutor was nervous, not happy about their prospects. He'd met the judges in chambers an hour ago, and they interviewed Senci, with all lawyers present.

"Xipe totec," Jaguar hissed. "What the hell did he say for himself?"

"Everything the judges wanted to hear, and then some. It's not looking good." But they'd soldier on. Court tomorrow morning, bright and early.

Somehow the rest of the day became evening. She called Alex and filled him in. He said he'd continue to watch, and she felt reassured knowing that. Alex, One Bird and Jake, they'd all be doing what they could, if anyone could do anything against the monster they faced.

She went to dinner with a tense Daro and even tenser Susan. Only Philip kept up the appearance of calm, and that angered her more than anything. As if he can pretend he's above it all, she thought. As if he can avoid feeling this.

After dinner, Daro turned his pinched face to Jaguar. "Can you read to me tonight?" he asked. Susan and Philip exchanged glances. Jaguar ignored them.

"What's your choice?" she asked.

He picked the life of Jackie Robinson. Jaguar curled up at the foot of the bed and read to him until he fell asleep, and then continued reading until her own eyes closed. She supposed she fell asleep there, because the next thing she heard was Philip's voice in the room.

"Dr. Addams? It's an early day tomorrow and maybe . . ."

She shook herself awake, stumbled out the door, and took a cab back to her hotel. She knew nothing else until the morning, when she remembered where she was, and why.

CHAPTER 10

SHE ENTERED THE COURTHOUSE ALONE. Daro and his family would not be there today. The new attorney was there, clutching his briefcase like a weapon against the horror this case had become. She slid into a seat next to him and whispered, "Anything new?"

He shook his head. "Not a damn thing."

Dr. Senci entered shortly after them, walked to his place and sat.

The judges walked in, everyone stood and was seated.

Dr. Bannur spoke.

"The Medical Protection Board has been placed in an unfortunate position, primarily through the irresponsible behavior of the Provincial Attorney's office."

The lawyer next to Jaguar stifled a groan. Dr. Bannur continued. "The material evidence in this case was unusable. The primary witness proved unreliable. And the attorney of record—" he paused, considered his word choice, "has passed away under suspicious circumstances, leaving a note which might indicate the entire case was fabricated. Therefore, this panel declares a mistrial. We abjure the Provincial Attorney's office from bringing such dismal cases to the Board and offer our apology to Dr. Senci. Doctor, you're free to go."

Gavel pounded against wood. The judges stood, and everyone else followed suit.

Jaguar clenched her hands at her side. "You didn't apologize to Daro," she spit out at them.

Three faces turned toward her and blinked.

"I said, you didn't apologize to the witness for the Province or whatever the hell you call a twelve year old boy who just turned himself inside out to try and do the right thing," she repeated loudly. The lawyer clutched at her elbow and she jerked away from him.

The judges whispered among themselves, then turned to her again.

"Who are you?" one of them asked.

"I'm Dr. Addams," she said, raising her chin high. "Dr. Jaguar Addams."

"Dr. Addams, you're out of order," Dr. Bannur said. The judges turned as a body and left the courtroom.

Jaguar continued to stand and stare as the lawyers left, murmuring something to her about telling Daro and his family. Something about the possibility of a retrial. She didn't move after they left, or as Dr. Senci shook his lawyer's hand.

He seemed as far away as hope, and so close she could trace the lines in his face with her tongue. He was miles above her, circling her. His breath was on her cheek.

When his lawyer was gone Senci walked across the room to her, stood facing her. But now he was different. He was a man in a white lab coat, and his hands were encased in surgical gloves. He held them up, showed them to her. His features shifted, became a face she knew from long ago.

Remember, Jaguar?

His eyes were a darkness she fell into. Her oldest fear lived in them, holding her close, and she understood at last why he was here. As she stood in bondage to his gaze, she saw the nameless horror she'd scented from the start.

"You," she whispered. "It was you."

Her childhood nightmare, her oldest enemy, facing her once more.

You know me. You know me. You remember.

She remembered.

When she was a little girl he'd walked into her grandparent's apartment, shot her grandfather and grandmother while she watched. His hands, encased in surgical gloves, tossed her across the room. His eyes stared down at her as he removed her clothes and pushed himself into her.

This man. His hands. His gun. His evil.

Senci, the Greenkeeper, who killed her family and raped her. He'd found her at last, as she always knew he would.

And you never saw me again from that day until this. Until this day, Jaguar.

Senci laughed.

Then, he gave her his profile, and he walked out the door.

* * * *

Jaguar left the courtroom feeling ready for vision or death.

Daro needs you, she told herself. Focus on Daro. Stay with him. Don't think about Senci. Not yet.

Don't listen to Senci, One Bird said. He lies, Jake said. But he didn't lie about this. She knew him at the exact moment he wanted her to, the memory stampeding through her, bringing its ancient pain.

Leave it alone, she told herself. There's work to do.

Before she left the courthouse she put in a call to Alex, and this time was glad to find him not at his desk. She left a message telling him what happened in court in the driest possible terms, telling him she'd be spending time with Daro before she came back. She didn't say what she knew of Senci. She couldn't.

"And you can stop the guard duty," she added. "I won't need it anymore."

She didn't mention why that was true. That was one other thing she couldn't think about. She turned her thoughts to Daro, and kept them there.

The attorney went with her to give the news to Daro and his family. Sitting in their beautifully appointed living room, he explained the meaning of the mistrial as opposed to an outright not guilty. They could try him again if new evidence turned up. That was the Court's way of telling Dr. Senci to keep his nose clean. At least they got that much.

Nobody talked about what went wrong with the voxchip or with Daro. Nobody talked about Clara. It seemed both pointless and exquisitely painful. Susan and Philip clasped hands, shut their eyes hard, then showed stamped-on smiles to their son.

"There," Susan said. "It's over. Now we can get on with our lives. Right, honey?"

"Of course," Philip said. He put a hand on Daro's shoulder. "Your mother and I were talking about a long vacation. Maybe to the States. To Florida. There's a Disneyworld there. We can stop at places along the way, see those big cats Dr. Addams told you about."

Daro stiffened at his father's touch. His face worked hard, then grew still. "Sure," he said. "That'd be great. I think I'll go lie down."

He walked away from them, down the hall toward his room. Jaguar followed and stopped him as he pushed open his bedroom door.

"Wait," she said, groping for words he might hear, wanting to hold him but afraid he'd feel that as a violation. "Daro, it's a mistrial. He could be tried again."

"We lost," he said, his voice expressionless. "We lost, and he won."

She touched his shoulder lightly, withdrew her touch quickly. "We lost this round. And it hurts like hell, if you ask me. But listen, you don't have to be afraid. I can—Daro, it'll be okay. Like I said, I can help you. I can stop him."

He shrugged, the gesture saying what she knew was true. She couldn't stop him from melting the voxchip. Couldn't stop him from getting free. "I just want to lie down, if that's okay."

"Sure. Of course. I'll stay for awhile, and we can talk later."

Jaguar allowed him his retreat. She stared at the closed door, then went and sat in the living room with his parents.

They could be nothing but quiet.

The room, neat and neutral, was surreal in the bright sun that poured in, in the sounds of traffic and people passing outside, in the sound of her own heart beating. Her skin was light around her bones, as if it would lift from her and fly away with very little provocation. Her eyes did not know what to look at, what to see.

She drew her lower lip through her teeth, preparatory to saying something. Anything. Just words to remind herself that she still lived.

"I'll stay the week," she said. "I think I can help with Daro. He needs to know he's safe, in spite of this."

"Mm," Susan said.

Philip patted her hand. "He'll be fine, once we get him away for a while. A good, long vacation."

She wanted to scream at them to wake up, but she felt wiped out by the possibility of exerting so much energy. She heard the sound of Daro's door opening and closing. It seemed closer than it could possibly be. As if she stood with her ear pressed against it. Then she heard him walking down the hall, away from them, out the back door.

He was probably going to the shed, a place he'd feel safe. His own place. She heard his steps as if they were pressed into her brain, and she frowned. Why was everything so unnaturally clear?

She tracked him with her mind, checking what signals he gave out. One Bird said stay close to him until it was over. Wasn't it over? No. Something was happening. Something else she needed to do for him. Don't leave him alone. Stay with him.

He was—something important. Something that shattered in leisurely violence.

"No," she cried, and rose from the couch, her legs striding out against a dense wash of time that collapsed around her.

Daro No

She lurched across the living room, knocking her thigh into the edge of a chair and thinking she would bruise from this. She struggled with the back door, her hands fumbling for the latch, finding it, pulling it back. She ran through the yard where everything was thick green, indolent green, slippery with recent rain. She stumbled, caught herself, slipped again as she fell through recalcitrant time. She thought she would bruise from this, thought, later I will be bruised.

Daro, don't. Daro don't. I won't let him get you Daro here I'm here I can help you.

The shed was far away, and then it wasn't. It was in front of her and she tried to push the door open but it was locked so she kicked at it. She saw each fragment as it splayed from the frame and shot out and away.

She stood inside the shed and saw

No, Daro I can help you I'm here I can help please no

Saw Daro at his worktable, holding his father's gun.

Time was so strange. Her vision so particular. She saw how big the gun looked in his hand and how young he was. She saw splinters of wood floating in planes of light that entered through the doorway.

He lifted his eyes to her, young eyes, baby eyes. His mouth formed words.

I won't let myself become him. Won't let myself become him.

Did Daro say that? Daro's mouth?

The words echoed around her. Her hand went out, trailing sluggard flashes of light as she flung herself toward him, reaching for the gun, her hand stuck in time in time *Daro no I won't let you won't let you do this.*

He moved deliberately, unhurriedly, knowing he had time because he'd taken all of time and left her none.

He pressed the muzzle of the gun to his forehead, and he pulled the

No. Daro don't Daro please don't

He pulled the

Daro no no no.

The trigger.

He pulled the trigger and it made a hole but only a small one, much smaller than his eyes so particular in pain, the mouth still saying *I won't become him won't become him I won't.*

Such a small hole surely she could close it up if she could get to him in time, in time. She reached and could not grasp as the bullet blasted through him, thousands of bright bone shards flying out like fragments of splintered doors, each piece of bone a jewel, a bird in flight away from her. She moved to him, thinking, if only I could catch the pieces, I could press them back together.

His eyes still open looked at her. Only at her.

Daro Daro, sweetheart. Don't don't don't do this.

She caught him as he dropped and she fell to her knees, his head cradled in her lap, her hands dipped in slippery blood and grey matter, her hands trying to hold him trying to reassemble

Daro sweetheart don't leave I can

Shattered pieces of bones piercing her hands and his eyes staring at her and he was

Stay with me Daro, please hold on

He was slipping away, his bones too sharp, his ghost too small to hold, his death dancing in her face, a wild and strange creature that caught like bones in her throat saying *I won't*

let myself become him. I won't become can't become him I won't

She cradled him in her lap, keening out a song of release as she felt the careening of his young spirit into an unknown universe that spun around them like the fury of lightning.

Then Susan and Philip stood in the doorway. They were yelling. They walked into the watery sea of her eyes, calling out blame. They called out blame, and Philip picked up the gun.

She dropped her hand from the back of Daro's skull and let it all fall down.

CHAPTER 11

WHEN THERE WAS NOTHING ELSE SHE COULD DO, Jaguar left the house without anyone taking notice. The parents were sedated, the officialdom of death still there. Relatives and lawyers had arrived, so she was superfluous. More importantly, the forensic people had the gun.

In the shed, when Philip and Susan found her holding their dead son, Philip looked like making more trouble, picking up the gun, pointing it at her, at himself, at his wife.

Jaguar, sitting in a widening pool of Daro's blood, was unaware that she was doing as One Bird instructed and chanting the prayer of release for his spirit, mint in her hand and death in her voice. Seeing them, she came back to real time with a shock.

"Put the gun down, Philip," she commanded.

He wheeled back to her, and she held his gaze hard.

"No," Susan gasped. She dropped to her knees and raised a sacrificial face to him.

"Do it," she pleaded. "Me first. Please, Philip."

He began to shake all over, and he dropped to his knees to embrace her, absorbing her sobs with his trembling body. The gun clattered to the floor of the shed and lay there, still warm.

Jaguar relinquished Daro's body, went and picked the gun up with the tips of her fingers wrapped around the edge of her bloody shirt and brought it inside. She made the necessary calls, waited for the necessary people to arrive, and then she left. Probably more cops would want to talk to her, but she didn't care. She had nothing of interest to say.

Without any conscious sense of how she traveled, she got herself back to her hotel room, where she caught sight of herself in the mirror. Her eyes were wild, and dark red stained her face and clothes, matted with Daro's blood. Daro's brains. Daro's death. That, she thought, must've gotten her a gasp or two on the streets, though she had no memory of hearing any.

She went into the bathroom, lifted her shirt over her head and let it drop into the bathtub. She pulled her pants down and checked the pockets. Mint, and there—at the bottom—Daro's earring. The small hoop with a tiger dangling off the end of it, its mouth open in a growl. She breathed in roughly. Pain danced in her veins.

She'd heard old people tell stories of something you could do in the days of combustion engines, if you hated someone. Put sugar in the gas tank of their car. It dissolved, made its way to the engine, and when the engine cooled it resolidified, gumming up the works. No matter what you did, it would continue to melt and resolidify in different places. There was no getting rid of it.

She put the earring in her own ear, finished changing, packed and left the hotel. She had one more thing she needed to do in Toronto.

* * * *

She took a cab to Dr. Senci's house, old and stately and large. She left her luggage in the back, told the cabbie to wait for her, and ascended his front steps.

She didn't knock, but just stood at the door and waited. In very little time he opened it and stood there. She didn't move or speak.

He studied her. Merely studied her with his old eyes. More than a thousand years swimming there. Thousands of years of death, all his. Then he clutched her face with the tips of his fingers, holding it still.

His grip was metallic, capable of cracking green bones. Within it she felt how old he was, how long he'd been doing his work. And she felt what he wanted next. A partner, to help him create the kingdom he desired. Someone with her particular strengths and talents to work with him. Someone he could subsume to his will in these matters. Inside her, something toxic moved from place to place, like sugar in an old car.

He released her and they stood staring at each other. She wondered if the cabbie was watching, and what he'd make of it all.

"You killed Clara," she said.

"Yes," he replied, voice flat and cold. It wasn't a topic that interested him.

"Why?" she asked.

He curled a hand toward her. "It's what I do, Jaguar. It's just what I do."

Of course. He was probably responsible for more cumulative death and destruction than nuclear weapons. An original template, one of the earliest of Greenkeepers. "But Daro—that was different, wasn't it?"

"That was for you. To call you back to me."

To call her back. A set up to get her attention, get her there. Daro's dreams, the trial, Daro's death. All that, just to get her here.

"And the little girl? That was for me, too?"

He nodded.

"Who is she? One of your kind?"

"Not yet. But she's good at leaving her body. I make use of that."

Not a spirit child after all, Jaguar thought. Another trick. "And how do you think you'll make use of me?"

"It's not use, Jaguar. It's possession. You are mine."

The hands, in surgical gloves holding a gun to her head. This man. A Greenkeeper old as time, pounding himself into her, binding her to him then letting her mature like a fine wine until he was ready to drink her in full.

You are mine you are mine you are mine.

Something toxic shifted to her throat and caught there. Breathing became a chore, and she focused on it until it felt like a natural action once more.

"You were afraid of me then," he said.

Her memory of that time was green as new grass. How quickly she taught herself not to feel. How quickly she understood that the worst evil was to become him, the worst mistake to feed him with fear or grief or pain. And when it was over, she'd embraced the fears that haunted the streets she'd walk as a ghost, a girl child who survived her own death.

"No," she said. "I wasn't afraid. You know that."

He narrowed his eyes at her. "And now? You're afraid now, aren't you?"

"Not of dying," she said, which was true.

He tilted his head back and breathed in through his nose, swallowed as if drinking her. "Not afraid of dying," he murmured. "Then what?"

She considered. When the worst had already happened, the time for fear was past. "I'm not afraid at all," she said. "Not anymore."

He wrinkled his nose, as if something unpleasant had been dropped into the stew he was sniffing. He raised a hand toward her, palm out. She tensed against it, closing herself, all thought, all emotion, contained in a space she held inviolable. She would not let him taste this.

She felt him pushing against her, this creature who cared for nothing but feeding and not dying.

She struggled with her body, feeling the life go cold and empty with his, and with great effort, she brought a hand up and slapped him hard in the face.

He stepped back, hissed. Testing. He was still testing his power against hers.

She laughed. "You can't have me by killing me, and you won't get me without killing me."

"You're wrong," he said. "You're mine already. I made you mine long ago. Now, I'll make you live that."

He reached down and grabbed her wrist, speaking inside her.

You will become me, know what I know, become what I am and live forever. So much you could do, so many children you could save. Think of it Jaguar. Think of it.

What he knew of power. All the time that was his. It could be hers. And perhaps in her hands it would be a different kind of power, wielded differently. It would be hers, wouldn't it? All the children she could keep from him. All the children she could save.

She knew what he was doing. He'd tested the stick. Now he was letting her sniff the carrot. Neither one interested her.

She jerked her wrist from his grasp. "If I do what you want, I'll feed like you. I'll *be* you."

His faced worked its way through anger and into another smile. "Everyone has to eat, Jaguar. Do you fault me because my food is different than yours?"

"Yes," she said, cold now, echoing Daro. "And I will not become you."

He laughed. "The boy is dead because of you," he said. "The boy, and Clara. If you continue to refuse me, who do you suppose is next?"

He moved his hand across her eyes and she saw the faces he already knew. Rachel. Gerry. Jake and One Bird. And Alex. Of course, Alex.

He couldn't kill her, but he could and would kill all she cared about to get her. He would go after all of them. Go after anyone she loved and kill them the way he killed Daro and Clara and she would be helpless to stop him. Unless she agreed to become him.

You can save them, Jaguar. Or you can watch them die.

Defeat settled into her. Any direction she moved was catastrophe. She'd fought him in her childhood, fought the results of what he did to her all her life. And he won anyway. He was right. She was bound to him.

She raised her face to his and he breathed in with deep pleasure, witnessing her defeat.

"Before I—" she stopped, started again. "I have some things to take care of," she said.

"You can settle your affairs before you come to me," he said. "I know how to find you. But don't try any tricks or you'll regret it. And don't take too long. When I'm tired of waiting, they'll start to die. Alex will be first."

He turned his back on her and went into his house, closing the door in her face.

CHAPTER 12

Planetoid Three—Toronto Replica, Zone 12

ALEX STOOD AT THE WINDOW IN HIS OFFICE, looking out and looking down. Looking for Jaguar. He felt as if he'd been standing there all of his life. Looking out and looking down. Looking for Jaguar.

She'd already filed her official research report, full of facts and absent any feeling. Daro was dead. Dr. Senci would not be coming to Planetoid 3. She'd made brief empathic contact with him, letting him know ahead of time what was coming, but even in that she stayed distant, official, clearly working hard to hold it together. He knew what shape she was in. Bad was the main word that came to mind. But he'd see for himself soon enough. She'd come back now. Her job was done.

She wouldn't forget, though. Like her namesake, she latched on until death. They'd have to come up with some way to get Senci. When she came back.

He looked away from the window and glanced at his computer screen, which listed his unfinished reports file. He swore softly, moved his gaze back to the window and stared out some more. The sky was blue and big, empty of intent or emotion. It carried no unfinished reports, no failed assignments or incomplete files on matters of the heart.

He left the window and took a seat behind his desk. Everything was normal. He'd get some work done while he waited for her.

His telecom buzzed and he picked it up. On screen, unexpectedly, he saw Jaguar.

"Hi," she said. "You got the report?"

He leaned forward on his elbows and studied her. Her eyes were dark with defeat. "I got it," he said. "How do you feel?"

"As if I've been taking a bath in a vat of toxic waste. As if I never want to feel anything again."

Reaching out to her, Alex felt the coldness that still surrounded her. It was the cold of willing relinquishment. The cold of the Greenkeeper. "Where are you?" he asked.

"Still in Toronto. Waiting for a flight."

"When will you get in?" he asked.

She shook her head. "That's why I called. I didn't want you to worry. I'm taking some time off."

Time off made sense, he thought. Time to heal, to cleanse the stink and ache of the case from her bones. If that's all it was, he'd be fine with it, but he knew her, so that was a fairly big if.

"Where will you go?" he asked.

"New York first," she said.

"Why there?"

"Because it's not here," she said. "Besides, it's a hub city. I can go anywhere I want from there."

"I'll meet you," he said. "I can get the red eye, I think."

"No," she said quickly, then added, "I—have to be on my own with this for a while."

He met her gaze and pressed hard against it. "Where will you go, Jaguar?" he asked.

Her mouth twitched. "I don't know."

"None of your plans involve Senci, do they?" he asked. "Because if they do—"

"I don't have any plans," she said, her voice tight and high. "I don't know what I'm going to do. I don't know. I don't know."

No lie in that. She was on the edge. "Okay," he whispered. "Okay. Just—remember you're not alone, will you? Call me. Let me know where you land."

She held out a hand, asking for a moment. He waited as she closed her eyes, pressed her fingers against her temples and breathed herself back to calm. When she opened her eyes her face had returned to its neutral position.

"I promise," she said carefully, "I'll call if you can help."

That was slippery. Something slippery, stalking the edges of her words, peering around her defeated eyes and neutral face.

"There's something you're not telling me," he said.

Lines formed on her forehead. "If there is," she said, "it's because I can't. Not yet. It—it hurts too much to talk about it."

"Then show me," he suggested, raising a hand toward the screen.

"I can't. I *can't* go over it again and again. Alex, please. Not yet. It would—it would kill me."

Looking at her face, he believed her. Nor would he risk breaking her just to placate his own worries. "How long will you be away?" he asked.

"I'm not sure. I'll—I promise you'll hear from me."

"If you want me," he said, "I'll be there in no time."

"I know," she said softly. "That I know. Alex?"

"Yes. I'm here."

"Thank you," she said.

And before he could respond, she was gone from the screen.

CHAPTER 13

DON'T FEEL, SHE TOLD HERSELF ON THE FLIGHT to New York. Don't feel anything. Just think. Do what you need to do. Just think.

She got out her notebook and concentrated on tasks. She considered writing letters—one for Rachel, and one for Alex—but decided against it. No telling what would happen if she started to write. Words were too dangerous right now.

Instead, she made arrangements to transfer her pension and savings to Rachel's account, postdating it four days. When Rachel got it she'd tell Alex and he'd understand the implications, so she had to make sure it didn't arrive until he could no longer find her, but also had to still be alive when the funds transferred or it wouldn't be legal. She sent a letter of resignation to Paul Dinardo on automatic email, also post-dated, using her name as the subject. When Paul saw it he'd take his time reading it, but she wouldn't be a Planetoid Worker when she went to Senci.

Finally, she sent an email to her lawyer, instructing him to deliver certain items to one Alex Dzarny in the event of her death. Something twisted in her chest, and she pressed a hand to it.

Don't feel, she reminded herself. Don't. Don't. Don't.

She couldn't allow herself grief. She had to think. Alex was safe. Rachel was safe. Now she had to get the job done. First, she had to figure out what the job was.

Should she give herself to Senci? Would that stop him? Heal him? If he fed from her, would her spirit enter his and heal him? Was it her task to let him become her rather than becoming him? And if not, what would she do? Kill him? But how?

Her knife would be no help unless she could get to his heart and take it. How she'd do that without his noticing and objecting strongly was beyond her. Poison was her best bet. Something that slowed him down enough that she could use her knife. But how would she get it into him? She imagined he'd sniff out any poison in food a mile away, and he was too quick to let her get a hypo in him or let her shoot him with the Cyanide bullets some weapons used.

If she couldn't heal him or kill him, was she to become his willing slave, living out her childhood nightmare for eternity, bound to him forever?

Davidson said, "Like the biochemicals that give Greenkeepers their name, the memory of fear is green, and its roots difficult of discovery. To weed it out takes a willing plunge into darkness and probable death."

That, she thought, was pure Davidson—lovely, brutally honest, and unhelpful. But it might also be the most accurate description of what she had to do next. A willing plunge into darkness and death, her only remaining hope that death was swift.

She stared out the window at the smallness of the earth below. She had some promises to keep before she did anything. She told Jake and One Bird she'd go to them. She'd keep her word.

She leaned back in her seat and closed her eyes.

Planetoid Three—Toronto Replica, Zone 12

Alex completed his work for the day in a state of numb precision, paperwork passing over his desk, people coming in and out and talking to him. He responded automatically, efficiently, and then turned away. No one noticed anything wrong in his carefully held eyes and carefully chosen words. No one saw that he was waiting for something he couldn't name. Rachel came in to ask if Jaguar wasn't supposed to be back today, and he told her she was taking some time off. Resting.

Rachel nodded sympathetically. It was a rough case, and Jaguar wasn't used to failure. Should she try and talk to her?

No, Alex told her. Not just yet. Give her a day or two. Rachel eyed him hard, but agreed.

When the day was over he went home, put himself into bed and slept as if he'd been hit with a rock. When the next morning rolled over him, he got up and did it again. And again. Somewhere at the bottom of his brain he knew he was waiting. He just didn't know what for.

He went through the week this way, working hard, avoiding Jaguar's friends, not returning calls from Gerry or Pinkie or Marie, not answering the questions Rachel had in her eyes. He couldn't act on an inarticulate foreboding, so he had no choice but to wait for it to take definite shape or dissipate.

Toward the end of the week, toward the end of another day with no news good or bad, he felt frustration mounting. He had to do something. He wasn't one to just react. He wanted, in some way, to act.

He picked up Dr. Senci's folder and read it again. It didn't tell him anything new and in anger he swept it off his desk, watched the papers skitter across the room. That was the best thing about hard copy, and probably why people still insisted on it. You could send it flying across the room when you were pissed off. You couldn't do that with electronic files.

But then he picked it up, brought it back to his desk and put his hand on it, breathed himself into quiet and asked to enter into his gift. The art of the Adept was to become aware of future possibilities. Sometimes the knowledge was metaphoric. Sometimes it was direct.

Today, it was nonexistent.

All he found was a longing for Jaguar, a desire existing so strongly in the present no future possibility mattered. When he tried for what would be he saw nothing except her face. Felt nothing except her hair wound in his hands, tasted only her mouth under his, sweet enough to wake the dead.

He gave up, and returned to the work of the day.

He was reading Teacher reports when his office door opened and Rachel appeared, closing the door behind her. Strange of her not to knock first. And she looked frightened.

"What?" he asked. "What's wrong?"

She sat down hard in a chair. "Jaguar transferred all her money to my account," she said. "I wouldn't have found it for weeks, but I lost my cash card and had to check my balance. There's—all her money, Alex."

He pressed a hand hard against the edge of his desk. "All of it?"

Rachel opened her mouth to speak but was silenced by the buzz of the telecom. She stared at it, then at Alex. He let it buzz. His machine would pick it up. He didn't want to talk to anyone.

His message kicked in, and then the voice of Board governor Paul Dinardo spoke.

"Okay," Paul said, "so earlier today I get this screaming call from personnel that a certain Dr. Addams transferred her retirement funds to another account—One Rachel Shofet by name. They say she hasn't filled out the proper forms, and it's screwing them up."

Alex laughed dryly. She would get that wrong. She was never any good with forms.

Paul's message continued. "Now I really wouldn't give a rat's ass about her retirement because I don't think she'll make it that far, but then I get an email from her, post-dated and delayed. It's a letter of resignation." Paul sighed deeply. "You wanna tell me what's going on, or you just wanna handle it? Lemme know, okay?"

Alex heard his machine buzz briefly and go silent. She had resigned. She'd given her money away. She was gone, and did not intend to come back.

He lifted his hand, made a fist, and brought it down hard on his desk.

"God *fucking* dammit," he roared. "God *damn* her to hell she's going after Senci."

"Alex," Rachel started to say, but he cut in.

"No," he barked at her. "No, no, no I will *not* chase her. I will not spend my life chasing after her disasters and evasions I will *not*. I will *not*."

He put his hand down to a clay bowl with a red feather in it that sat on his desk. He picked it up and drew it back as if to fling it across the room.

Rachel gasped. Alex stopped his motion, stared at the bowl.

It was a gift from Jaguar, a sign of her willingness to share who she was with him. He wanted to break it. He couldn't.

But she'd lied to him. One more time, she'd lied.

Then, he thought, no. She hadn't. As usual, she was a lousy liar, but the master of evasion. She'd asked him not to ask. She said it would kill her to tell him, and that he'd hear from her. All absolutely true.

She also said she'd call if he could help. She hadn't called, which meant she thought he couldn't help, and there was the real problem.

She was going against a Greenkeeper. For once, she might actually be right.

Rachel cleared her throat. "Book a seat on the next shuttle?" she asked.

"Yes," he said. "And if there's no seat, kill someone. Get their ticket."

He put the bowl back on the desk and left his office. He had to get ready to go.

CHAPTER 14

Home Planet—New York City, USA

Dr. Senci stood in his Penthouse Apartment staring out the window at the city below. Then he threw his head back and bellowed into the night.

He had a pain in his body.

Pain coursed through his head in a ribbon of motion and landed squarely at the back of his eyes. He squeezed at his temples and bellowed more.

He didn't like pain, and in the absence of wounding, he shouldn't have any. Not for another two centuries at least, when this form might begin to show wear and tear that even feeding wouldn't heal. Then he'd have to go through the tedious process of replacing it a few bits at a time, reconciling each bit to his core energy and shaping them to his peculiar genetic qualities. It was like feeding, except that it required access to at least four bodies simultaneously, and it could take months to complete. The bodies he used had to be alive throughout, so finding a place to work was a problem, because people chosen for the honor generally made a lot of noise.

But he had pain, and he shouldn't unless he was being wounded and if so, who dared wound him? Someone gave him this pain deliberately. Who?

He sniffed the air. A soft static scent, like something burning, filled him. Sage, he thought. Burning sage, giving him a headache.

He uttered an oath and slammed a fist against the hearth. He should be scenting Jaguar. Where was she? He'd tracked her easily enough when she left Toronto, heading toward Manhattan. He'd followed her here, bringing the children, thinking she might choose to meet him in the city where he'd first bound her.

But she'd stayed only briefly and then moved on, going to her old village in New Mexico. He hadn't pursued her. Not yet. He could afford to be generous, let her say her goodbyes. But once she arrived there her scent was gone, hidden by whatever tricks those people she called family knew. Now he had a pain, and smelled burning sage.

He held a hand out for her, wanting to grab her and shake her, throw her off a cliff. If he found her he could do that easily enough, even at this distance. His hand touched nothing. She was gone. Just gone.

Rage became a song inside him. She was gone and he had pain. If this was her feeble attempt to escape—well, she'd learn not to try again.

Of course, it might not be her. She had powerful guides. Powerful friends in that old village. Perhaps they worked for her. If so, they'd soon learn the consequences of such stupidity.

He walked over to his window and peered up at the sky, which was clear and to his eyes showed the edges of the Milky Way in misty relief against the blackness of night. The Planetoids were invisible in the darkness, but he knew her friends were there. He'd find one.

He tried for a different scent. One that meant something to her. Alex. He sent out a thought to connect them. A thought of Jaguar. Part of her they both knew.

As he made the connection, he twisted his gaze back down to the earth below him. He'd found something interesting.

Alex wasn't on the Planetoid. He was on the home planet, headed for New York.

Senci smiled.

Alex was on his way. The children could deal with him. They knew what to do. When they were done, he'd have one less pest to deal with, and Jaguar would see that he meant business, in case she didn't know it already.

"Now where is Peter?" he muttered to himself. He went in search of him, and of the girl, to begin the process of reeling in his prey.

Home Planet—New Mexico, USA

The sun danced to its accustomed spot on the horizon, glowed gold and then bled its life out over miles of turquoise sky. Jaguar saluted it and walked down the dusty, unpaved road that lead into the canyon and to Jake and One Bird's village, 13 Streams.

She'd taken a cab to the top of the road, wanting to walk the rest of the way. She carried only a backpack with some clothes and a bottle of water, and that was heavy enough. She still felt the energy drain of the Greenkeeper, still carried something toxic in her veins. Each step was a burden, even though she walked toward a place she loved.

Her mother grew up at 13 Streams, and Jaguar lived there until she was five and her grandparents took her to Manhattan, over the objections of Jake and One Bird. They said she was too wild for anything except wilderness, and they were right because ultimately she found the Planetoids—the wildest place of all.

But when she told herself the truth, Jaguar knew this village was the one place where she could openly be all of who she was, and she'd have to return here again and again to renew herself if she wanted to continue her work. It was the only place that accepted all her disparate heritage.

One Bird's father, a Mayan shaman, had settled here after he ran from Guatemala with a price on his head during one of the wars there. Later, well after he died, other Natives showed up and ultimately they laid claim to a swath of land through one of the treaty reparation acts made just before the Serials. Now a few thousand families lived here, some Native and some not, planting their food, holding ceremony, operating businesses.

They came from many places, especially during the Serials when word got out that One Bird took in strays. City Skins began to show up, leaving urban areas destroyed by murder, by diseases from biobombs and too many bodies piled up in the streets. Others came from reservations, looking for city friends and relatives they were worried about. Then non-Natives from suburbs came, seeking escape from a spiritless world. One Bird took them all in. 13 streams of people, which meant everybody and the unaccountable, mysterious, one more than everyone.

This was her vision, she told Jaguar. Her work in the world. And Jaguar belonged here, where all those who belonged nowhere else chose to live.

She rounded the last corner of the road and saw the village just ahead, its adobe houses almost seamless with the land around it, growing out of the rock and sandy soil. As she passed them, people would note her arrival, but nobody would come out to greet her. That would be pushy, rude. Tomorrow, if it seemed right, those who wanted to see her would slowly begin to gather around.

She came here twice a year at least—once for a sweat to clean out any residual shadow she fielded from her prisoners, and once for the sun ceremonies her grandfather had started here long ago. She supposed this place was as close as either she or her grandfather ever came to having a home. As close as their wandering would allow, because more than anything, the Mertec tradition was one of wandering.

Their name meant the walking people, those who kept going, those who went up. Going up the land. Going up the rivers. They were, their stories said, attracted to upward motion. Jake often said that explained why she went to the Planetoids.

The Mertec had lost much of their tribal identity as they followed their wandering tradition and their ways mingled with others, but Jaguar could still spot someone who probably came from her line. A certain fetish on a Zuni necklace. A scratched out image of a jaguar's open mouth with a hummingbird inside. Knowledge of certain herbs. These told the genetic tale, though there were few full bloods to talk about it.

If rumors about her father were true, half her blood wasn't native either. She once overheard an old woman ask her grandmother if she was the little girl that Spaniard left behind. Others whispered about her as the daughter of a cougar man. She was both a motherless and fatherless child.

"Stop feeling sorry for yourself," she muttered under her breath. "Jesus, you're disgusting."

The truth was, she'd always have a home at 13 Streams, and she couldn't ask for a better one. Even the Planetoids didn't fully embrace her the way this land, this people did. Here, all her empathic arts were taken as natural, part of the way the world worked. Some people had a talent for healing, some for growing good corn, some for speaking with the spirit world. What was called psi capacities or empathic arts on the Planetoids and the rest of the home planet was called simply medicine here. There was no need to categorize or explain it, and they didn't understand why anyone would make a fuss about it.

When she got to Jake and One Bird's house she stopped, stood and stared at the smooth adobe walls, let herself adjust to the energy. Let the house adjust to hers. Though they were the elders of the village, their house was no different than others except for the glyphs of sun and moon carved in the door. Those glyphs told all.

What this old couple knew of the spirit world was beyond any naming. Their skills in the empathic arts were so much a part of their being they couldn't name them as separate from themselves. What they did was who they were, and all of that was good. Jaguar had been infinitely fortunate to learn from them.

When she felt she'd waited long enough, she opened their door and went inside.

One Bird was washing dishes at the sink. The radio was on, playing something jazzy and fast, and she sang along, her broad shoulders lifting and falling in rhythm as she worked, her long grey braid swinging back and forth against the back of her brown cotton housedress. Jaguar watched, staying still. One Bird kept at it until all the dishes were clean. Then she wiped her hands on a towel and turned from the sink, still singing.

When she saw Jaguar, her mouth clamped shut. The dark eyes in her wrinkled face grew wide. She recited some choice words in Tzutijil, snapped her fingers to turn off the radio.

"Hello, One Bird," Jaguar said, leaning a hand on the adobe wall to steady herself.

"I'll get Jake," she said. "Sit down." She moved past Jaguar and left the house, seeking the old man.

Jaguar didn't trust herself to get to the chair. Walking here was as much as she'd reserved energy for. She slid down to the smooth floor and sat, held on to the wall and waited. A river of pain washed from the top of her throat to the bottom of her spine. She ached everywhere, and found it difficult to breathe. The Greenkeeper at work, killing her slowly until she returned to him. And even with all their skills, what could Jake and One Bird do about that?

She rubbed a hand against the wall, listened to the idle buzzing of a fly in the room. Just under the surface of this wall were the remnants of etchings she'd carved when she first got here after the Killing Times. Jake let her use his penknife to make them, he and One Bird watching her as she cut her grief and rage into images in the walls.

After a few years here they gave her a bucket of adobe and paint to fill them in, paint them over. By then she was ready to do so. And as she worked, they watched her, saying nothing. They were very good at watching her, and saying nothing.

Sometimes their silent watchfulness drove her crazy. She wished they'd just say what was on their minds, not leave her guessing if she'd done something wrong or if they were about to pounce on her. Then she realized they were saying what was on their minds. She'd forgotten how to hear anything but screaming since the Killing Times. They were reminding her that quiet still existed in the world. That not all silence was dangerous.

They were always teaching her something in that way, and all of it was useful. They taught her how to find barriers and clear them with a touch and a breath. They taught her how to cleanse herself after contact, keep herself from eating shadows. They taught her the rituals of thanksgiving, grief and praise. They taught her ways to feed the spirits, hungry for human gifts, for beauty, laughter and tears, love and rage.

And they taught her which gifts were hers. Chant-shaping. Clearseeing. Naming truths. The gifts that got her in so much trouble. The gifts that brought her here.

Jaguar smoothed the wall and thought of Daro, smoothing wood. Pain coursed through her and she stopped her hand. What images would she carve here now?

She pushed the button at her wrist that released her red glass knife into her hand. She pressed it against the wall but went no further. She had nothing to write on these walls today, and there were better uses for her knife.

In the Mertec tradition, if you were either filled with grief or about to relinquish your life, you cut your hair. She reached across her shoulder and grabbed at the braid going down her back. She held the knife close to it, not sure what her intent was, perhaps just testing for the feel of it.

Did she mean to die? Did she have a choice?

The front door creaked open and slapped shut. She turned, knife and braid still in hand, and saw Jake standing in the entrance, One Bird right behind him.

"Stop that," he said.

She stared at the knife but didn't move. He walked to her, pressed the button that retracted her weapon, pushed her hand down. He stood over her, his sharp features tight with anger, his arms crossed at his chest, waiting.

She spread her hands out and stared at them. "Jake," she said, "I'm in trouble."

"Yeah," he said. "I can see that."

She was dusty and dry as the bones of the earth. She carried the scent of the dead on her and they smelled it. He removed his hat and ran a hand along the dome of his balding head. "You need to lie down," he said.

Jaguar thought briefly about arguing, then dismissed the idea. He had something he wanted to accomplish with her, and she had a promise to keep. She pushed herself to standing, steadied herself against the wall.

"Okay," she said. "But can we keep it on white man's time? If I delay, people might die."

"It'll take what it takes," Jake said. "Go. We'll be in."

She walked out of the kitchen, into the cool, dim light of the hall toward the room that was hers since she was a teenager. She ran her hands against the thick adobe walls, felt how solid they were. They grew out of the earth they stood on and retained the comfort of their mother. As she entered her room, taking the required step down into it, she heard Jake and One Bird talking quietly, each in their own language. That meant it was serious talk. English was for every day.

The room was sparsely furnished. A mattress on a wood frame close to the floor. An old bureau. A table made of a round slab of a tree, balanced on a stump.

The two long and narrow windows let in slants of the remaining day's light at exactly the angle she remembered. She let her hand pass through it, let light play on her skin. Then she went over to the bed and lay down, turned to her right and ran a finger along the wall where she'd carved the outline of the animal that shared its name with her. It was the only carving she hadn't covered up.

She was tired, but she couldn't fall into sleep. Whatever Jake and One Bird had in mind, she hoped it didn't take too long. She was safe here, protected by a cluster of some of the most powerful empaths you'd find on the planet, but they couldn't protect Rachel or Alex. Or Alex.

His name—just saying it—opened a channel of pain in her chest. She breathed herself away from it, afraid of the depth she might fall into, never to find her way out. She could be trapped in this hole in her heart, and if she feared anything, it was being trapped.

As if she was not trapped already. As if she had any good choices left.

The sense of someone in the room rather than any sound made her open her eyes. It was One Bird, alone.

"Where's Jake?" Jaguar asked.

"Still pissed off. He's gotta get over it."

"I didn't mean to—"

"Don't worry about it. He don't know everything. He just thinks he does. Besides, he's gotta make the offering. We'll start without him." One Bird's soft hand touched her face. "You're pretty sick. You know that? Full of poison, and someone stealing your breath."

"I know." The sucking sensation in her chest wouldn't go away.

"You been having dreams?"

Jaguar nodded. Dreams where she stood on the mesa and Alex stood with her. Where she stabbed him, and he fell. The inexplicable triumph in his eyes.

One Bird grunted. She pressed her lips tight together and hummed to herself. Her hands moved over Jaguar's face.

"You're sick from grief, too," she said, speaking more gently now.

"From Daro and Clara," Jaguar whispered, and felt the throbbing of pain.

"More than that." One Bird pressed a finger to her jaw. Jaguar winced at the touch.

"He wants me to become him," she said. "To—to be his."

One Bird shook her head. "Doing what he wants won't work."

"Then maybe if I let him feed off me, he'll change."

"No."

"He says—"

"He lies."

Simple, and clear. He lies. Becoming him would save no one, and giving herself to his feeding frenzy wouldn't change him. She was relieved and disappointed simultaneously. A part of her hoped her sacrifice would somehow redeem what happened to her grandparents, to Daro, to Clara. And in a stolen moment between willing sacrifice and death, she might allow herself to feel love, something he'd taken from her long ago.

At this thought, a wave of sorrow moved into her and stuck around.

"There," One Bird said. "That's what else you're grieving. Like a river in you. An old river."

A hand moved from her head to her throat. She choked as it tracked the course of her despair.

"You don't understand. I have to—I have to figure out what to do. There's no time for this."

"We have to get the poison out first," One Bird said patiently. "You're no good to anybody until we do."

Jaguar shook her head. No. This was too much. She couldn't.

You have to. Breathe, One Bird commanded. *Open.*

Jaguar had years of trusting that voice. She complied. Her awareness lowered through her throat, to her chest, past her heart and into her belly. It lingered there, sensing darkness and—something else. A thin thread connecting back to her heart.

One Bird began to sing, her hand hovering over Jaguar's body as her awareness traveled the road of her spine, clearing out cobwebs of fierce guardedness and whatever else she thought kept her safe. Jaguar felt new toxins and old energies breaking up, passing through and out of her as she breathed deeply and slowly.

Stay open.

Her awareness moved back up into her head like wind circling inside her, clearing out the dust. Then, back down through her throat and into her chest, to her heart.

Her heart.

One Bird's hand lingered here, letting Jaguar feel what lived there.

Hurt. It hurts. Can't breathe.

Through the pain she sensed One Bird's impatience. She knew better than to turn her face away from the truth.

Don't struggle. Just fall. Let yourself fall.

She turned to her grief as if she loved it, as if the slow light, resonant and soft, would carry her away away away from herself. But it didn't. It only turned her back to this trap she called a hole in her heart.

I don't want to feel this.

It's yours, Jaguar. It's just you.

It's awful.

One Bird laughed softly.

No. It's all there is in the whole world, and it's you. Own it.

Jaguar struggled for breath.

I'm dying, she said.

Do you choose that?

Was that her choice? Did she prefer that to her grief? She didn't fear death. Maybe she didn't believe in her own death enough to fear it. Or maybe she'd seen too much of the world of spirit to see death as fearful.

But no, she didn't choose it. Not yet. There was something left for her to do before that. Still, what she feared most was in the living rather than the dying.

What do you fear?

Jaguar breathed through the twisting knot in her chest. What she saw was Alex. Just Alex.

If I love him he'll die like they died, like he dies in my dreams and I can't I can't let him die can't bear to live with that grief without him without him.

Yes, One Bird said. *Your fear.*

Her fear. That her love would be death to Alex, to anyone she loved. That his death would destroy her. That there were some losses even she couldn't survive with her spirit intact. That she was someone whose feelings ran so deeply such a thing could destroy her. Afraid of love. Always afraid of it.

Now you know, One Bird said. *Now you know.*

But what difference did it make? How could it help her or Alex or any of the people Senci would kill to get at her?

What do I do? What do I do?

She felt something like a sigh move through her.

You know. Let the love be bigger than the fear, Jaguar. See who you are. Be what you see.

One Bird's hand moved over her, and Jaguar felt the tearing release as she entered emotions she'd hidden from for so long, in so many ways. Without anything left to stop her, she fell like a stone dropped into the bottom of a canyon, into something that felt nearer to death than to sleep.

Home Planet—New York City, USA

New York, Alex noted, shone and sparkled in the night, clean and easy and ready for anything. Though it had 3 million people less than before the Serials, it still could seduce you with its rhythms, its passions and glory.

Alex walked down a street where pretty young people moved in groups of threes and fours, laughing, heading into clubs, emerging from cafes that stayed open all night. He was heading toward the cop shop and their computers where he could track recent registration to hotels and recent airline travel by fingerprint code. He'd called ahead to let them know a Planetoid Supervisor wanted their help, something the Manhattan cops in particular were responsive to. And if he couldn't find her that way, he'd have to find her another. But find her he would. Preferably, alive and kicking.

When he found her, he'd kiss her. If he found Senci first, he'd try and kill him. He might as well. He'd already given his life over, handing in his resignation just before he left.

He stopped at a corner and read the street sign. There used to be a good bar just a few blocks from this corner. A place with sawdust on the floor, where you could get a hearty beer in a dark room without anyone trying to pick you up or look you over. He made his way to it and found it still existed. He elbowed his way to the bar, slapped down his money, and ordered a pint.

When the bartender brought it and he was raising it to his lips, he saw a flicker of something in the bar mirror. A flicker of something unusual. Golden, and spotted with the eyes of the night.

A golden jaguar, raising a paw to her mouth and licking it.

She lowered the paw slowly and looked up at him.

He turned away from the reflection and toward the crowd. The jaguar stood and sauntered to the door. Nobody saw her except him.

"Okay, then," he said, and put his beer down, pushed his way to the door and back to the streets.

He looked left and then right, saw her still sauntering in a leisurely way down the street, invisible to everyone except him. He followed, staying well behind. She turned down a side street, and he sped up, turned the corner and saw her still there, still leading him on. Then, she took another corner into an alley, trotting now, and he trotted, too, quickened his pace to a run as she began to run, went down the alley she leapt into, saw her golden fur catching some unseen source of light that made her glisten in motion.

He followed at a run down the narrow lane, keeping his eye on the light glinting off her fur in the night.

I choose you, she said.

Then, he heard laughter. Laughter, like that of children making mischief. Abruptly, he stopped running and listened. The voices of children reached his ears. Girl voice. Boy voice. Girl voice again.

"Stop it," girl voice insisted haughtily. "I told you how we're doing it."

"Think you know so much." Boy voice was petulant.

"I got him this far, didn't I?"

Alex peered into the darkness at the end of the alley. The jaguar was gone, but there, at the end of the alley, a little girl and little boy faced off. His fists were hard at his side. She had her hands on her hips and tapped a foot. He'd seen that gesture before. Seen that stance before. It was pure Jaguar. He wondered if Jaguar would recognize the boy stance as his.

For the first time in days, he smiled.

The boy shrugged and walked away, and the girl turned to Alex, walked toward him. He waited, not moving or speaking.

When she stood directly in front of him, she said, "You're looking for Jaguar, aren't you?"

"I am," he admitted.

"Then come with me," she said, and walked back to where the alley met the street, humming as she went. He followed, and in attending to her he forgot to pay attention to his back. So he was taken completely by surprise when something hard came down with force on his head.

He fell for what seemed like a long time, into a place of absolute darkness.

CHAPTER 15

HER KNIFE PLUNGED INTO ALEX'S CHEST, AND HIS EYES WERE TRIUMPHANT.
Jaguar pulled it out, felt the sucking of the wound as he fell to his knees. Voices moved through her, asking questions.

Do you want this, Jaguar? Is this what you want?

But then there was screaming. Someone wouldn't stop screaming, a sound like metal on metal amplified twenty times. It was awful.

"Jesus," Jake shouted over Jaguar's screaming. "She makes a lot of noise." He kept his hand pressed against her throat as the horrid sound erupted volcanically all around them.

"It's the poison," One Bird shouted back. "She's full of it. I'll get more sage."

As soon as she left the room Jaguar's eyes flew open, though Jake knew she wasn't awake. She cursed him, swung at him. "You *fucker*," she screeched. "I came here to feel better you fucker, I hate you I hate you I *hate* you."

Jake chuckled softly as he held her arms down. "Good thing you don't know how weak you are," he said. "You'd be *really* pissed off."

One Bird returned, bearing a clay bowl filled with loose silver leaves. She held a match to it, let it catch, then sang as she used a feather to spread the smoke over Jaguar.

"People are getting a little worried," she mentioned when the song concluded. She jerked her head to the side, and Jake looked out the small window, where a group had gathered.

"Tell them to make a fire. Get a drum circle going."

One Bird frowned at him. "Do we need it?"

"It'll drown out the noise," he said.

Once again she left, and Jake took the glass of water at the bedside, dipped his finger in it, then passed his fingers over Jaguar's eyes, her lips, her throat. He lifted his hand, ran it lightly over her chest.

The screaming subsided into a moan. One Bird returned with a basin of fresh water and bathed Jaguar's face with a wet cloth.

"That's better," she said. "She stopped fighting."

"For now," Jake said. "Don't count on it lasting. I wish she'd shed some tears, though. She'll need them."

One Bird put a hand on her forehead and followed Jaguar's now silent journey as she was drawn down and down and down to a place smaller than a coffin, where she had to crouch, bend low, her shoulders crushed against her knees.

A coffin, trapping her, getting smaller and smaller. But she couldn't get any smaller. Couldn't be smaller than she was. Her face was pressed to the bottom of the box, the weight crushing her and only a small hole to breathe through.

"Come on, girl," Jake encouraged. "Don't stop here. Keep going. "

She flattened herself to the hole and asked herself to become her breath and leave this place, flow out of it, not smaller, but different. Instead she was reduced to her skeletal self, emerging without skin into the world she longed to leave, her bones angry and restless. She reached out for something—anything—felt her bony hand grasp the warmth of another beating heart. Wrenched the heart from its casing of rib and flesh and held it high. As it beat in her hand she sang, and flesh flowed over her. Her moaning grew louder, soon rose into a wrenching cry of pain.

"Hurts, does it?" Jake asked, and continued to smooth his hand over her heart.

One Bird brushed smoke over the area. "Keep going," she admonished. "You know what's next. You gotta cry it out."

Outside, the drumming began and they could smell pinyon and sage smoke, someone cooking a hot dog. Jaguar writhed and cried out, but she shed no tears.

"She don't cry easy," Jake noted.

"She needs to," One Bird replied. "You know why."

Jake rubbed a hand across his face. "Yeah. We got any tequila?"

"I'll check."

When she returned with the bottle Jake took it and poured some into his hand, then smoothed it over Jaguar's forehead, her throat, her chest. One Bird put her hand back on Jaguar's head and witnessed what happened within.

Jaguar stood on a mesa, Alex facing her. He pulled her close, kissed her.

Now? Now, Alex?

Now is what we have, he replied.

Jaguar, alone and filled with tearless grief, stood outside of desire as if it were a house she wanted to either occupy or destroy. But she couldn't beat the door down with her hands and she couldn't run from it with her feet and she couldn't stab it with her knife so she stood still and listened.

Listened to her heart beat out this song.

Simply listened.

In Jake and One Bird's dirt and sagebrush yard more people gathered around the fire. As Jaguar's voice rose into screaming and subsided into silence, drumming wove in and out of the night and the drummers turned to each other and nodded. It was a good sound. It went with healing. Within the house Jake and One Bird continued their task while night turned itself into morning. At dawn the people dispersed, only to be replaced by other people, all willing to work the drum.

The song went on. The healing continued. The morning turned itself into day, and the day turned itself into night.

Finally, One Bird wiped her hands on a towel and stared down at Jaguar. "I think that's all we can do," she said.

"Shit," Jake said. "No tears. Not one. She's gotta have some tears."

"The poison's left her, and she knows a thing or two she didn't know before. Maybe that's all we get. Maybe she's gotta find her own tears."

"Yeah," he said. "Maybe."

"We should let her rest. Real rest."

Jake ran a finger down the side of her face and spoke to her softly in Zuni. She murmured in response, automatically. Her breathing shifted, and the lines on her face smoothed into true sleep.

When One Bird and Jake emerged from the house they looked spent, but they nodded at the people who circled the fire.

Gaiwayo, someone in the circle said. A Seneca woman. *Gaiwayo*.

All is well.

One Bird agreed. She brought out a pot of stew, a basket of bread. Coffee and water. Everyone drank and ate.

Home Planet—New York City, USA

Dr. Senci emerged from the hotel feeling better, but still very hungry. His feed had relieved the pain in his head, but she had died while he was still sexing her. That was pleasant, but not filling enough. He needed more to satiate his energy needs. He would gather as much energy as he could before he went to Jaguar.

He walked down the streets to a section of the city where working women still plied their trade. They eyed him as he strolled their ranks, assessing their chances for a good night's pay. He assumed his most appealing aspect and returned their stares, making it clear he was looking to hire one of them. Before long a woman in a short leather skirt and halter top grabbed his arm.

"Want some fun, mister?" she asked.

He considered her. She was thin, but for him that wasn't a bad thing. It could mean she had higher energy levels, and what he ate was energy, not flesh. "Perhaps," he said, smiling, and caressing her. "You were offering...?"

"Good times," she said, and snapped her gum at him. "Right this way." She crooked a finger, sauntered off toward a building. He followed, though he wasn't sure if any sexing would truly satisfy him anymore.

He wanted Jaguar. Wanted her. The closer he drew to having her, the more anxious he was to own her completely, make her fully his.

"You got something big on your mind, Joe?" The woman asked. He blinked up, and saw that he was in a bedroom with her. He had no memory of coming here, but that wasn't unusual. He often lost time, since it meant so little to him.

"Yes," he said, "something big."

She peeled herself out of her tight clothes to reveal unnaturally large breasts in a red bra. "I like big," she said. "Show me."

"Come here," he said to her.

"Okey doke," she said cheerfully and joined him where he sat on the bed. He unhooked her bra, cast it aside, pressed his mouth to her nipple and sucked.

Sucked deeply.

"Hey, that's special. That feels—hey. What the hell?"

Her voice wavered. He sucked, and looked up at her face, saw her eyes roll back in her head. He braced a hand at the back of her neck but she slid down onto the bed and passed out.

He stopped his feed, felt at her neck for a pulse. It was weak, but it was there. He'd wait until her energy returned just enough to bring her to consciousness, then he'd feed more. She'd be frightened, already knowing she was about to die. That would make for a good feed.

He calculated it would take her about fifteen minutes to revive, and while he waited, he turned his thoughts back to his apartment. He sensed nothing wrong. All was quiet there. No surprises. Then again, the children were used to being on their own, since he often left them alone so he could hunt. They knew better than to misbehave, and right now they had something special to keep them occupied.

He searched and felt the presence of the little girl, heard her contented humming. Alex was there with her, unconscious, and she was guarding him carefully just as instructed. Peter was impatient to start on him, but the girl wouldn't let him. She had her instructions and she'd follow them to the letter.

He'd promised her a horse if she did exactly as he asked, and she was looking forward to getting it. Not a pony, though, she'd insisted. A real horse. White, with a dark star on its forehead. He'd agreed.

Now, sensing her compliant satisfaction, he knew he could take his time to feed here, returning home tomorrow or even the next day. Then he'd watch the children play with Alex before he consumed him. As an Adept, he'd make a particularly good feed.

The woman on the bed gasped, opened her eyes. She sat up hard and tried to stand, but fumbled it. He grabbed her arm, pulled her back onto the bed. She clawed at his face and he smiled. A little scuffle was nice now and then.

He let her get on with it, allowed her to feel some hope of escape because that would intensify the flavor of the meat. Then he shoved her hard onto her back and put his mouth to her nipple, getting his teeth into it this time, drawing blood and drinking in earnest.

It was good. Full of the energy of flight. Full of fear.

After a while she began to spasm, her hands flailing out at nothing then clutching at her throat. He lifted his head and watched her face, saw the bursting of blood vessels behind her eyes. He went back to her breast and continued to suck until she was drained dry. Then he bit off the end of the nipple and swallowed it.

He licked his lips. Not a bad feed. He decided to find at least one more. A young one.

He patted the dead woman on the leg and left her there. The next one he would sex first, and then feed off of. Perhaps it was old fashioned of him, but he preferred it if those he sexed were still alive.

* * * *

When light returned and vision with it, Alex found himself prone across a round bed covered with deep red satin, his hands and legs bound by steel cuffs. The bed was soft, and the satin slippery, but he managed to elbow his way up into a sitting position and look around.

The round bed was in the center of a large and well-proportioned room with a domed ceiling. Inset lights played on the mirrored walls. Pictures of people in a variety of sexual acts adorned them, and on a low bureau sat statues of Chinese erotica, all in jade and gold.

"Great Mother," he said to himself. "Where the hell am I?"

The oak door creaked open to answer him, and a group of five children, ranging in age from perhaps eleven for the youngest girl, to maybe sixteen for the oldest boy, filed into the room. Two boys and three girls. They approached the bed, keeping a safe distance, and stood staring at him.

"He's alive," the oldest boy said.

"Of course he is, Peter," the youngest girl said. "He's supposed to be, isn't he?"

"I thought we got to kill him," one of the middle boys said. He pushed his face forward and sniffed Alex as if he might smell bad, then pulled back and stood silently picking his nose.

The girl he'd spoken with in the alley stepped forward and slapped his hand. "Don't do that," she said. "It's gross."

She walked closer to Alex, looking him over. "Does your head hurt?" she asked.

"Not too bad," he replied. "But thanks for asking."

She creased her forehead as if she didn't understand what he said. Not much courtesy in her life, he supposed.

He kept his gaze on her, making surface empathic contact. He found thoughts and emotions older than her years, and something on her mind that had nothing to do with killing him. Something she was keeping well hidden from the others.

He turned his contact from her to Peter, who was hollowed, scooped out. Nothing of self left. Just a hole, waiting for Dr. Senci to fill him.

And the younger boy, who had a rage bigger than all of them put together. And the other two girls, who were soft in the middle, gooey, already worn out of their souls.

It didn't look good.

Peter stepped forward and pushed the girl out of the way. "Who cares how his head is? Let's have some fun with him."

He put a hand on Alex's face, turned it to profile, then back to full face. He let his hand drop into Alex's lap and rubbed at his crotch. Alex gulped air hard and pulled his legs up to block him. The little girl laughed, and Peter glowered at her.

"What's your problem? Aren't we supposed to sex him? Isn't that what *he* said to do?"

Alex, keeping his knees drawn tight to his belly, decided it was time to become a real presence. "Hey," he barked at them, and they all jumped. "Where am I, and what're you up to?"

Peter started to speak but the girl interrupted him. She seemed to hold some authority with the group, even greater than this oldest boy. "No, Peter. We only sex him right before we kill him. You know the rules. Now go away. I'm supposed to talk to him alone."

The children looked angry, but they left, and Alex slowly lowered his knees. The girl stood staring at him, her wide dark eyes giving nothing away. Alex waited.

"You know her," she said without preamble.

Alex shook himself. Know her. "Jaguar?" he asked.

The girl nodded. "I want you to tell me all about her. Everything you know."

Alex took in breath and let it out slowly. "Are you Maya?" he asked.

She startled. "Who told you my name?"

"Jaguar. She talked to me about you."

"What did she say?"

"That you were smart. Tough. That you needed help. That you led her to Daro."

The girl nodded solemnly. "Dr. Senci wanted me to, but that's not why I did it. I thought if anyone could help him, she could. But now she's gone, and Dr. Senci said we should kill you to bring her back. Peter'll bring a gun in, and I'm supposed to shoot you in the legs. Then the others get to sex you. If you don't cooperate, I kill you. If you do, he'll feed off you when he gets back. He'll do that to all her friends, if she doesn't come."

She recited the litany as if she was telling him to do the laundry then wash the dishes then if he didn't mind could he walk the dog. He supposed it was a familiar routine to her. Dr. Senci's preferred method of sex. Immobilize, rape, feed and kill. Not his idea of a good time.

"Maya," he said, "Is that what you want to do?"

"I don't know yet." She wrinkled her nose in distaste. "I don't like the sexing part, but Peter does. I just want to know about her."

Alex breathed out slowly and thought about what he should say next. The truth, he decided, would be a good place to start.

"Dr. Senci's using you to trick her, to make her be with him," he said. "When he finds her, he'll kill her, and I can't let that happen."

This was apparently too complex a thought for her. She twisted her lips around, pulled at them, let them go. "I thought she was his queen," she said. "She's supposed to come and be—my mother."

"Is that what Senci told you?" Alex asked.

She nodded.

"He lied," Alex said.

Maya went close to Alex, sniffed the air around him. Testing him for the truth? He supposed so. She must have some pretty good empathic capacities to be able to project an image of herself so clearly. He had no doubt she could, Jaguar-like, smell what was real.

She did. Her face went bright red. She turned and kicked hard at a chair behind her. "That Cocksucker," she screeched. "He *always* lies to me. He's such a liar. I *hate* him."

"Then," Alex said, "why not leave him?"

Her leg stopped midkick. She brought it down to the floor, swiveled around to him. "Leave him?"

"That's right," Alex said. He raised his hands. "Undo my cuffs. I'll take you and your friends out of here. We'll go find Jaguar without Dr. Senci."

She considered. "The others might go, but I don't think Peter will. He wants to transform, and Dr. Senci promised him."

"The others that were here? What're their names?"

"I don't know," Maya said. "I didn't ask. I don't like names. I only use Peter's because he makes me."

"But he doesn't know your name, does he?" Alex said.

"Of course not. And don't you tell him either, or I'll kill you."

"I won't," he said, and he meant it. He wondered where she learned that bit of ancient wisdom. That your name carried power and to keep it secret was to preserve its power. A strange child, but a wise one. Now she seemed lost in thought. She hummed tunelessly and stared up at the ceiling.

"Where's Dr. Senci?" he asked at last.

She continued humming, and shrugged. "You know," she said. "Hunting."

Hunting. For more children. For a meal. An ex-cop told him once that he knew more than one pedophile who referred to children as meals. He wondered how many of the pedophiles they had on the Planetoids were ex-meals of Dr. Senci's he didn't finish off.

"When will he be back?" Alex asked.

"How should I know?" She was irritated with his questions, as if they interrupted her line of thinking. He fell silent and she went back to her humming.

When she brought her attention back to him he raised his wrists. "Uncuff me, and we'll leave," he said.

She frowned. "I'll think about it," she said, and, ala Jaguar her queen, she turned and left the room.

CHAPTER 16

Home Planet—New Mexico, USA

JAGUAR STUMBLED INTO CONSCIOUSNESS to the sound of something like spoons clattering against plates. She was hungry. She smelled food. Heard food. She opened her eyes to darkness in her room.

It took her some moments to locate herself in space, remember where she was. Then she pulled herself up, noticed she was still dressed in the clothes she'd arrived in. She stood and made her way clumsily out of the room, down the hall and into the main part of the house. Nobody was here, or awake, but outside she saw a leaping light and heard a crackling. Someone had a fire going.

She also heard voices, Jake's among them. She walked to the door and opened it, saw Jake and two other men she didn't recognize sitting on stones placed around a small fire. An empty pot of stew stood next to the fire, with a pile of used bowls and spoons next to it.

The other two men looked at her, at Jake. Then they got up and left.

Jaguar walked over to the fire. "Was it something I said?" she asked.

Jake narrowed his eyes at her. "Stop bullshitting."

"I don't know what you're talking about."

"Then who does? The Mailman? Should I go ask him?"

She sighed. She should know better. Jake never did small talk when big talk was around. "How long was I out?" she asked. It looked like deep night, a sky cast about with stars. "What time is it?"

Jake checked the stars. "About four."

Almost a whole night's sleep, which was more than she'd had for awhile. "Not too bad," she muttered.

"Yeah," Jake said, "A few days sleep probably did you good."

She blinked at him. "Days?"

"Yeah. It's four am, Friday."

"Friday?" She was appalled. She'd arrived on a Tuesday.

"You went under," Jake said.

Under was right. Under the bottom of the universe. Under the bottom of herself and then some. She remembered some of it, like dreams that continue to hang around, holding more feeling tone than sense. But Friday? She'd slept that long?

"Jesus, Jake. You let me go three days? Senci could be killing people. I can't—"

"He's not," Jake cut in. "Sit down."

She contained her fury, took a seat on a rock, subjected herself to his gaze.

"That's better," Jake said. "Now tell me what you think you're in such a hurry to do."

She struggled for words. What was she going to do? The problem was, she didn't know. "I need to find Senci, and—and stop him," she said, trying for a certainty she couldn't quite achieve.

"Not yet," Jake said firmly.

"Not yet? Then what? I let him kill everyone I love? Alex and Rachel and you and One Bird? I let him keep destroying children, creating more destroyers just like him?"

"Shut up," Jake said. "For once, just shut up and listen."

She retreated, sullen and silent. Jake swore softly and picked up a stick from the side of the rock he sat on. He used it to draw spirals in the dirt at his feet. She watched them take form and grow, living pictures he'd wipe out as soon as he finished them, going on to the next, making his magic as he spoke.

"The monster you hunt is a creature you don't understand, and can't redeem or destroy," he said. "He's been here longer than you can imagine. He's like you only in the smallest way. He has blood. He has a heart. He breathes."

She listened in the way he'd taught her, not just hearing, but also feeling what he felt as he spoke. She sensed an energy that was totally unfamiliar, even though it was housed in the most familiar of physical forms. Senci, the Greenkeeper, was a new color of evil, and she'd have to grasp what that meant if she wanted to get this job done. But Jake already understood him, and suddenly she knew why.

"You met him," she whispered to Jake. "You—journeyed to him." Jake grunted in acknowledgment. He'd done the shamanic journey that allowed his spirit to find Senci's and know it in its most essential form. A new possibility occurred to Jaguar: Jake could do the journey again and take her with him. Then she might learn what she needed to complete her task.

"Show me how to find him," she said. "Or take me to him. Let me journey with you."

"No," Jake said. "You're too close. It would destroy you."

"Anything I do will destroy me—"

"—Not that way. It won't work. Just listen."

She sighed, and stopped arguing. He wouldn't lie to her about that. "Okay," she said. "Okay. So what *can* I do?"

Jake wiped out all he'd drawn and began again, this time carving jagged edges in the earth. He didn't speak, but instead offered her his experience with Senci in wordless communication. She felt his energy, the anomaly of the purely negative. And energy couldn't be destroyed. It could only be shifted, transformed into something new. A combination of elements, the synchronicity of planned events and random occurrences was necessary.

Yes, Jaguar thought. It made sense in her mind, but she couldn't grasp what he meant in particular terms, couldn't feel it in her heart. Access to that intuitive center was currently not available. Jake, feeling the block between them, made a sound of frustration and snapped the stick in two.

Jaguar jumped at the sound. "Jesus, Jake," she said. "Can't you just tell me how to stop him?"

"I just did. You can't hear it."

"Then tell me another way."

"You're stubborn, you know that?"

"I learned it from my elders," she said pointedly. "So what do I do?"

He sniffed, scratched at the back of his neck. "While you were asleep, what did you dream?"

Scattered images, blips of feeling, returned to her. Dreams of Senci pushing into her little girl's body. Dreams of ropes tangled, holding her to him. Dreams of Alex, dead at the end of her knife. Dreams of hundreds of snakes circling her.

"I dreamt about Alex," she said, speaking carefully. She had to tell the truth, but she didn't have to feel it. "About killing Alex, and Senci killing me. And I dreamt about snakes. Lots of snakes."

"What does that tell you?"

She shrugged. "Alex is in danger. I'm in danger. We're caught in something tangled and big and poisonous."

"That's all?"

"Yes."

"Then you can't even hear yourself. You got any idea what you actually want?"

"I want," she said crisply, "what I can't have."

"That's what you think. And maybe that's why you can't hear what you need."

She stifled her frustration, her growing panic. Jake wanted something true from her and either couldn't or wouldn't help her until he got it. They'd done this kind of thing in the past, the two of them butting heads over questions she asked that he would only respond to by making her find her own answers. She made herself stay calm and considered her next words carefully. When she felt ready to speak, she stood and walked to him, taking one of his hands in hers.

"Jake, I know I'm not being as—as clear as I should be," she said quietly, "but we'll have to work around it, because I don't really matter here. What matters is that there's a great evil walking in the world. It happens to be the evil that killed my family and would like to annihilate any good I've ever known, but it'll do a lot worse if it's allowed to continue. You journeyed to him, so you know what's at risk. All the children, all the good men and women who'll die, all the souls he'll mangle and lives he'll shred. And my own life is worth nothing if I sit back and let that happen. I have to stop him, or die trying."

Jake spat onto the earth. "But you don't know how," he said.

Jaguar shifted restlessly. "No. I don't."

"And you expect me to tell you?"

"Something this important, I want your help," she said, "but I'll go on whether I get it or not."

Jake stood and turned his face up to the night sky, listening to the star talk. He and One Bird had never been overly protective of her. She was a warrior woman. That was her way and they accepted it. She didn't know why he was reluctant to help her now. Maybe he already knew she couldn't possibly succeed. That if she went after the Greenkeeper, she'd end up dead, or worse, and Senci would continue in his destructive path. Maybe he didn't want any part of that.

He scuffed his foot against the earth, then swiveled his head around to her. The intricate pattern of wrinkles on his face became deeper as he narrowed his eyes. "You dreamt about snakes," he said. "So ask them."

Then he turned and went into the house, leaving her alone to consider the talk of stars, of her heart, of snakes.

* * * *

Home Planet—New York City, USA

Alex sat on the bed, then lay down. Then he sat up again. There was nothing much else to do. Outside his room, he heard the children's voices rising and falling, sometimes petulantly, and other times in laughter. He wondered what they were doing. It sounded as if they were playing a game. Monopoly, maybe. Cards.

Dr. Senci's children. He collected them, in all five flavors. How many had he fed on? How many had he bound, who later became pedophiles and serial killers? Davidson said if you killed a Greenkeeper, the ones he bound or transformed died with him. How many would that be? And how many more would he destroy before he was stopped. Not Jaguar, Alex thought. Not her.

He looked around the room, saw there were two windows. Then he looked down at his wrists and ankles. Bound with plastic cuffs. Bound to Senci and his children, who might do anything. Their innocence made them capable of such evil.

The voices in the other room quieted and Alex tensed, waiting to see if something would happen. Nothing did for quite some time. Maybe they'd just gone off to bed.

He lay down, and closed his eyes, tried to imagine ways of releasing himself from his cuffs. He wasn't chained to the wall, so maybe he could leave them on and climb or jump out the window. He was about to raise himself to hop over and check when the door opened. He lay still, kept his eyes closed.

Footsteps crossed the room. Pressure next to him told him someone was sitting on the bed. Then, a hand moved down his side, found the button on his pants and fumbled with it. He lay very still, considering what moves he could make. He'd settled on a very intrusive and unempathic upper cut to the chin, followed by a little neural anomaly known in slang as St. Vitus' interruptus, when the hand stopped its motion.

"Peter," a voice said crossly, "I told you not to."

Alex opened his eyes. Peter's hand jerked away and he stood, pointed a finger in Maya's face.

"You can't tell me what to do," he barked at her. "You're not in charge here. You'll never be in charge. I get what I want, and I want to sex him."

"Dr. Senci'll be ma-ad at you," Maya said, sing-song.

"Then when do we get to kill him?" Peter demanded.

The noise brought the other three children into the room, yawning and stretching. "Are we gonna do it now?" one of them asked.

"Be quiet," Maya hissed to the little boy. "Go get the gun."

Alex sat up. "I thought you wanted to leave with me. I thought all of you wanted to leave."

"If she leaves, we'll tell on her. We already told her that," one of the girls said. She looked to be about twelve, scrawny and lifeless in a white nightgown.

"No," Maya said. "Nobody's leaving." She turned to Alex. "I thought about it, but it's not a good idea. They'd tell, and Dr. Senci'd be mad when he found me. Besides, he promised me a horse if I got you."

"A pony," the other girl corrected.

"No. A real horse. A white one," Maya said.

Alex sucked in breath and held it. The young boy walked back into the room holding a laser fire weapon by its muzzle. He lifted it to Maya.

"No," Peter said. "Give it to me."

"It's my job," Maya said. "Dr. Senci said so." She wheeled away from him and grabbed the gun from the little boy's hand.

"All right," Peter said, "But I get him first."

"Wait," Alex said, not sure what he was going to say next. But Maya wasn't listening.

She aimed the weapon at his leg while Peter stood picking at his fingernails. A shot in each leg. Then sex. Then death. He'd have to hurt her and he didn't want to. The thought of delivering a kick to a little girl's face was repulsive.

"C'mon," Peter said. "Hurry up, will you?"

Alex searched rapidly for her thoughts. Found only a heart beating very hard, a ringing sound, a small voice speaking larger than it had any right to, saying *Now Now Now. Do it now.*

She made a choking sound and turned the weapon on Peter, firing directly into his face.

Alex gasped, and Maya stood very still while he dropped like a stone to the floor.

The other children didn't move.

"Whadja do that for?" one of the girls whined. "He was gonna take me skating tomorrow."

"Shut up," she said, her teeth clenched. "Shut up or I'll kill you, too. *Shut up.*"

"That's enough," Alex said, staying calm. "We'll leave now. Uncuff me, and we'll just leave."

"I'm gonna tell," the boy interjected. "I'm gonna tell and Dr. Senci's gonna be mad. He'll probably eat you, but first he'll—"

Maya whirled to him and fired once, whirled on the girls and fired again and again. She kept firing until the children were dead, blood pouring out of them in many places, eyes vacant.

She lifted her face to Alex's, her pupils dilated, her face blanched, her jaw clenched hard. She let go of the gun and it clattered to the floor. She made a sound like howling withheld. She began to shake all over, dropped her face into her hands and crumbled into herself, sobbing.

Alex stood, remembered his ankles were cuffed, and dropped to his knees hard. He felt the jolt, but didn't attend to the pain. As best he could, he drew Maya close and petted her head.

"It's over," he said. "It's over now. You're all right. You'll be all right."

* * * *

Maya uncuffed him and they left the house together, walking out into early morning mist and humidity. The air was thick today. Heavy and thick. Maya said Senci might not come back for days, so they had time to get away.

Alex held her hand and led her. She seemed like glass ready to break. He wondered what damage this had done to her soul, and if she'd ever recover.

They walked without any sense of goal or direction for a few blocks, the only important thing to put space between themselves and the house. Then, Alex stopped at a corner, crouched down and put his hands on her shoulders.

"Maya, look at me," he said.

She blinked, eyes still wide and blank.

He brought two fingers to her forehead and gently asked permission to speak with her this way. Inside her was a roaring of emotion. He couldn't soothe it. He could only listen.

She had to leave. Had to get away. And they weren't going to let her. They'd already argued it out in the living room. Peter told her anyone who left was dead. The other children said they didn't want to go. They said they'd kill her if she tried to leave. Maya had seen enough killing in Senci's house to know they meant it.

Okay, he whispered into her. *You'll be okay. I'll take you somewhere where you can get help. A family. A mother.*

But where? He still had to find Jaguar. That was still the most important task, and he couldn't take Maya with him. Couldn't just leave her here.

He stood, looked up and down the street. There must be a Child Welfare House somewhere in this city. He could call information and find the building, bring her there. Explain that she'd been traumatized and needed help.

"Maya," he said, "I want to take you to someone who can take care of you."

She shook her head. "I want to stay with you. *She* trusts you."

She. Jaguar. "Dr. Senci's looking for me and for Jaguar," he said. "You'd be safer somewhere else. You know that."

"If you bring me somewhere else, I'll just run away."

"To where?" he asked.

She looked around, then pointed west, toward a scouring sun. "I'll go that way," she said. "That's the way Jaguar went, isn't it?"

He frowned. As a little girl, running from the horror of Manhattan, Jaguar pointed herself west and got herself to New Mexico. To Jake and One Bird.

For the first time since this mess began, his gift worked for him, sending him a clear vision of Jaguar standing in a field of sage, raising her face to a southwestern sun. Her thoughts circled images of him, images of knives and snakes rattling in the dusty earth.

"There," he whispered. "Of course." She'd been speaking with Jake and One Bird about Daro. If she wasn't there now, Jake would know where to send him next.

He took Maya's hand and pointed them in the direction of an airvan stand. "Ever been to New Mexico?" he asked.

CHAPTER 17

THE SUN PIERCING THE SKY WAS A BLESSING Jaguar had forgotten, as was the clean and clear scent of sage it lifted into the air around her. She breathed it in to the bottom of her lungs as she walked with One Bird and collected the herbs she needed for her various medicines.

Around them, the wind-smoothed cliffs and the close huddled groups of boulders at their base spoke in whispers of their business. The trail they walked, packed hard by many feet, was dusty. A dry spring had become a dry summer, and the people were worried about their corn and beans. Jaguar felt dry as the earth herself.

"You want this?" she asked, pointing to a clump of paintbrush.

One Bird turned toward her, considered, then shook her head. "Wrong moon." She walked on, and Jaguar followed.

Yesterday they'd completed a sweat and all her visions were of snakes. After the sweat, Jake pressed a finger against the corner of her eye and shook his head. He said stay another day.

She didn't want to. Being here gave her an illusion of safety that no longer existed. Listening to One Bird sing bad jazz as she washed dishes and chant for the corn as she walked the land, watching Jake scream invectives at the Dodgers when they lost the ball and make the morning offering at dawn—the familiarity of their daily gestures made it seem as if she'd returned for good to this place that sheltered her so completely. As if the Serials and the Planetoids were dreams sandwiched around what was real.

This. Here. Gathering herbs under the widest sky, the warmest sun.

She would lose her nerve if she stayed much longer, but she couldn't leave until she knew what to do, and so she stayed another day.

As they collected the gifts of the arid earth she remembered that the last time she walked here was with Alex, more than a year ago, the two of them collecting sage to bring back to the Planetoid. She'd come home for the summer sun ceremony and brought him along, wanting to share this place and these people with him.

He fit in easily, his innate courtesy leading him immediately to the right words and gestures for the occasion. The people in the village recognized him as a skilled empath, sensed both the steely strength and subtle vision that belonged to the best Adepts. She'd been proud to claim him as her friend. Proud to bring him here.

She remembered all that, then realized too late that memory was dangerous right now.

Sorrow passed through her like a sword, and suddenly her legs wouldn't hold her up. She sat hard on the ground, trying for breath and not finding it. She'd never known before this how physically painful grief could be, how it clutched at the heart with taloned hands. She wrapped her arms around herself and lay down against the warm earth, waiting for it to pass.

One Bird walked to her and stood nearby, listening to her ragged breathing, the sobs she wouldn't let rise from her throat.

"What?" Jaguar groaned at her. "What is doing this to me?"

"You gotta give in to it, Jaguar. You know that." One Bird said, and walked on.

It quickly became clear to Jaguar that she didn't know how.

Instead, she stayed where she was for a long time. It was comforting to allow herself this physical collapse without fear of anyone walking by and thinking her insane. A simple gesture, to lie with your face on the earth and feel your heart beat out pain.

The grit of the land moved under her cheek and the cool and prickly scent of sage filled her. A snake curled past her, paying her no attention. Nothing dangerous. Just a little whipsnake. If it was a rattler, she would have grabbed it and let it bite her heart and have done with it. Then let Senci find her. He'd feed off her, and he'd be eating poison before he knew it.

And as she thought this, every other concern went away.

"Snakes," she said out loud. "The snakes." She sat up fast and brushed the dirt from her face. At last, she understood.

The Greenkeeper avoided snakes, Davidson said. The venom invaded them systemically, couldn't be easily or quickly healed. Enough venom would certainly make them more vulnerable to other wounds.

Her dreams of snakes. Her sure knowledge of loss. Her profound grief. And in spite of what it meant, she felt triumph because at last, at last, she had something she could do, even if she died doing it. She lifted herself up and walked back to One Bird, who noticed the change immediately.

"Answers come easier when you're not chasing them down, don't they?" she said.

"They do," Jaguar agreed.

One Bird didn't ask for further explanation. From the look of sorrow on her time worn face, Jaguar figured she already knew.

* * * *

At supper that evening Jaguar told Jake and One Bird that she knew what to do, and was ready to leave. She didn't elaborate beyond that, and they didn't ask her to.

"Tomorrow," Jake said. "You can go then. There's one more thing you gotta do for me."

They left her in the house while they walked under the stars, and Jaguar knew they were consulting about her. She was causing them sorrow. She would cause them more. She had no choice. And if they needed a night to absorb that, she would give it to them. They'd given enough of their nights to her.

In the morning, Jake woke her early. The cool of night was still in the air, the sage and grasses dotted with dew that would dissipate quickly.

"That all you wear on your feet?" Jake asked, looking at her thonged sandals.

"That's all," she said. It was an old battle, trying get shoes on her, and they'd never won. The formula was familiar and comforting. A kind of love song they sang to each other.

"What about the snakes?" Jake asked.

"What about them?"

He shook his head, "Come with me."

"Where are we going?"

"To the garden. You gotta help me with beans."

"Jake," she protested, "I'm leaving."

"I told you there was one more thing. Beans first. Then you go."

They walked to the field where the corn was tall, and the beans turned their leaves away from the scorching sun.

He handed her a short hoe and a basket and sat himself down on a rock, opened an umbrella over his head, and pointed toward a row of bean poles. "Gotta weed it out, then pick. Start there," he told her, and she did.

The sun emerged fully, and in little time her back would have been drenched with sweat except that the dry air sucked it from her skin as soon as it formed. Her water bottle was empty by the time she went from weeding and hoeing to picking. Jake sat under his umbrella and watched her. He hummed to himself, occasionally closed his eyes.

When her basket was full she held it up for him to view. "Is that enough?" she asked.

He shook his head. "One more row."

She sighed and bent to her task. She reached around a pole that was heavily vined, picked a handful of beans and dropped them in the basket.

"You missed one," Jake said.

She looked over her shoulder at him. "Where?"

He pointed a bony finger to her left. "There," he said.

She stretched for it, found it just out of her reach. In pushing herself forward just a little further, she lost her balance and fell, chin first, into the dry earth. Behind her, she heard Jake chuckling. She cursed soundly, pushed herself up, grabbed the bean and pulled it down.

"Here," she said, standing and holding it out to him. "Happy?"

His grin lacked nothing but a few teeth. "You forget how to pull beans in that place you work?" he asked.

"Yeah," she said, "I've been busy."

He scratched at his hip and regarded her with his earth brown eyes, the wrinkles around them deepening as he squinted in the bright sun at her. "You forget everything else I taught you, too?"

He was enjoying this immensely, she thought. "Jake, get someone else to pick the beans," she said, brushing off her pants. She picked up the basket and walked out of the garden, toward the fields of sage between them and their home.

"No, no," he protested. He closed his umbrella, left his rock and trailed after her. "You gotta do it. It's part of the plan."

"The plan to keep me here for a year or so? It won't work. I'm leaving today."

He reached out, put a hand on her arm. She halted, turned to face him.

His eyes were sorrowful, seeing everything. "You gonna go this journey?" he asked.

"I am," she said.

"Tomorrow?" he asked.

"Today," she said firmly.

He took his hat off, pulled a bandana from his pocket and wiped his head, then put his hat back on. "You're not going alone," he said.

"Yes I am," she replied. "I'm going today, alone, and it will be a good day to die."

When she was nineteen she went back to the city to collect whatever remained of her grandparent's goods, gathered up in the general wreckage of the Serials. They didn't want her to go. Jake particularly spoke against it. But she went, and while she was there she ran into the cop who saved her life in Manhattan. He was already working on the Planetoid, and he brought her there to see it. She ended up back at school in the white man's world, and then working on a star, as Jake called it. Now she was back here, telling him she would die. Maybe, she thought, he'd been right about that trip back to the city.

Jake stood facing her. "Tell me how you'll stop Senci," he said.

"Jake, you don't want to know that."

"Maybe not, but I need to," he insisted.

She'd wanted to spare him the painful particulars, wanted to spare herself the pain of naming them to someone she cared about so much. She steeled herself and spoke as dryly as she could. Just the facts.

"The snakes," she said. "I'll milk them for their poison and inject it in myself. When Senci feeds off me, he'll eat their venom. And he'll die. We'll both die."

There was nothing else to say, so she was silent. She understood why he couldn't tell her this. It would be the same as advising her to kill herself, and it wasn't his place to do that. Not his place, and it would break his heart.

He rocked on his heels for a moment, staring at the ground. Then he lifted his gaze and studied her carefully. "Remember that story I told you about the directions of power? It's from the Lakota."

She nodded. "There's seven directions of power, and the seventh is the most powerful.

"That's right. Creator had a feeling humans might abuse that power, so he wanted to hide it. He asked all the animals to help find the right place. Eagle said she'd take it up to the sky, but creator knew people would get there pretty easy. Bear offered to hide it in her cave, but creator knew people would dig in there fast enough. Then, the little blind mole had an idea. Remember?"

She swallowed. Something about this story tugged at her. She had a vivid memory of the first time Jake told it, when she came back from New York after her grandparents died. She'd refused to sleep inside because staying out under the stars somehow felt safer. Jake came out, brought her a blanket, and told her the story.

"I remember," she said. "The mole told creator to hide the power where people wouldn't think to look, a place only a few people would dare go to."

"That's right," Jake said. "But the ones who took the journey would know the right way to use the power. So the most powerful of the seven directions was hidden inside the human heart. And that's where it still is today."

Her power was not in what she feared. That just appeared powerful. Her power was in what she loved. To know that was easy enough. To live it was something else.

"I still have to go," she said quietly.

"I know," he said. "Mary Hawk will sweat you this afternoon. Don't forget to give her something. You can leave tomorrow."

"Today," she said.

He shrugged. "Tonight. Do the sweat first. You got an idea where to go?"

"I'll take suggestions."

He pointed toward the canyon. There was sacred land out there. She knew it well. "Lots of snakes on the Mesa next to Sundagger. You can milk them," he said.

"Okay," she said. "I'll go there."

He pressed a gnarled hand to her cheek. "I won't see you again before you leave," he said.

She wouldn't see him again. Never again. She bit at her lip to chase away the deeper pain.

Tears slid down the furrows of his face. He wouldn't hide them. They were his gift to her, but she had none to offer in return.

He turned, and started his slow and hobbled walk toward home.

Home Planet—New York City, USA

Senci squatted at the corner of an alley and rubbed his head. Even in Manhattan, nobody paid attention to this kind of behavior. Nor would anyone notice the teenage boy lying in the dumpster behind him, his final feed of this hunt.

He lifted his head and sniffed the air. He'd been in this alley before today. In his endless circling of space and time, he once stopped here to feed. He searched through his memory threads, seeking the moment.

Yes. A good taste. A pleasurable feed. A youngish girl who had not consented, but who had died well. Nice to call it back. But he had work to do, and couldn't linger in it for very long.

He pushed himself up from the ground and walked toward his home. He had to remind himself to pay attention to time. He wasn't accustomed to doing so, but he'd never hunted anyone like Jaguar, and until she truly became his ally he had to be careful. He didn't imagine she could kill him. She was strong, but she didn't have his years, his capacities, or his experience. There were very few ways to kill him anyway, and none she could do alone. But she might elude him for longer than he wanted, and he was hungry for her.

When he reached his home he stood on the front steps and sniffed the air. He smelled blood. That was good. A good sign. It meant the children were already playing with Alex. The shots to the legs, the sexing, had already begun. He entered the building, stood in the hall and sniffed some more. Definitely blood. A lot of it.

"Peter?" he called. No answer.

He followed his nose, followed the scent of blood, which led him to the bedroom. He opened the door.

Alex was not there. Instead, the swollen, dead bodies of his children lay on the floor. All of them. No—not all. The little girl was missing.

Rage gathered in his belly. Alex was gone. The girl was gone. His other children were dead. He raised a hand and lowered it, tossing out his fury.

The bodies smoked and disappeared. He raised his hand again, not sure what he'd hit this time.

Then, he realized. Of course.

He could find the girl. She'd been with him long enough that he could do so easily. And Alex would probably be with her. He could find them both and toss his rage at them from where he stood. It was an exorbitant expenditure of energy, but well worth it. He'd smell them burning from here.

He raised his hand high, seeking the girl, but something stopped him. A call, faint and weak at first, then growing stronger.

Jaguar, calling to him.

Leave them alone, Dr. Senci. I'm waiting for you

He lifted his head. She was far away, but she wasn't hiding. In fact, she was leading him to where she waited, in an arid land where she appeared as if she'd fallen from a strange star to that place.

"Yes," he whispered, and felt a thrill of anticipation, so unusual.

Home. This was her home, where her power grew from. And he could feed on her where her power was greatest. Then, he frowned, considering a new thought.

This land and its people were protective of her. He needed to proceed with caution, make sure she wasn't trying to trap him in some way. He'd approach her carefully, move toward her in stages, and it would take a little time. But he had all the time in the universe at his disposal. That well never ran dry for him.

Ready, Jaguar? he asked.

Whenever you are, she replied.

CHAPTER 18

ALEX BROUGHT THE AIR RUNNER IN to land just outside the ring of adobe houses that squatted in the shade of the mesa.

"Well," he said to Maya, "we're here."

She peered out the window, pressed a small hand against the glass as if that would help her see better. "This is where she lived?"

"That's right," Alex said. He opened his door and got out. Went around to her side and opened her door, helped her out.

"Is she here now?"

"I don't think so," Alex said, "But I hope we can find her from here."

Alex had been here before and knew the protocol of the people and the place. He stood with Maya, letting the area adjust to his presence before he walked toward the houses. He saw people looking out of windows, staring at them. One head emerged, disappeared, then reemerged. Alex went to the center of the circle the houses formed and stood, holding Maya's hand in his.

"What're we doing?" she whispered to him.

"Waiting," he replied.

Soon he saw movement inside the house he wanted. The flick of a curtain at a window. He walked forward, to the door. It opened and an old man was visible, an old woman at his side. Jake and One Bird.

Alex stayed where he was. He read relief, but very little surprise in their faces. They'd been waiting for him. They were glad he was here.

They stood facing each other silently. When enough time had passed for courtesy, Alex nodded at Jake.

Jake returned the nod. "It's been awhile," he said.

"It has."

"Since the sun ceremony, year before last."

"Yes. Since then."

"You come all the way back to give away stray kittens?" Jake asked, indicating the little girl at his side.

"No," Alex said. "I'm looking for Jaguar."

A click of time passed. One Bird and Jake turned to each other and a conversation ran between their eyes. One Bird seemed to come out of it ahead of Jake.

"Come inside," she said. "It's time for supper."

They entered the cool interior. Maya stayed quiet, eyes large. She was taking it all in.

One Bird and Jake set out dishes and food. They ate and spoke of local matters. How the gardens grew. What happened to Kerodon's truck. How the rains were late this year. Nobody brought up Jaguar, but Alex could feel her recent presence everywhere. He reined in his questions and let Jake and One Bird lead the way.

After they'd finished dinner Jake pushed his chair back from the table and held a hand out to Maya. "I know some people who'd like to meet you, if you're willing."

Maya rose and put her hand in Jake's. She stopped briefly at the door and waved over her shoulder at Alex. He waved back and sighed—in relief or in sorrow, he wasn't sure—at her departure.

"There's a young couple here don't have any kids yet," One Bird said. "They'll probably have their own soon enough, but they want some in the house now. They're good people. They'll teach her the right ways."

"I appreciate that."

"She'll be fine. This is her home now."

"I know," Alex said. "So does she."

One Bird pointed down the hall. "You can sleep in the room down there. You'll recognize it when you get there. It's Jaguar's."

* * * *

Alex passed the night impatiently. Dreams woke him twice, and once awake he had to work to remember where he was. He kept feeling Jaguar close to him, then realized it was her residual presence, so clear in this space which was so like her. Delicate and sparse as fire. Durable as earth. Extravagant and simple as jade. Pure stone, waiting for water or fire or both.

The next day, he saw Maya sitting in a circle with three other children, watching them play a game with small round stones and smooth sticks. Once or twice she tried to jump in, but they silently rebuffed her attempts. She sat back and watched. They weren't unfriendly. They just wouldn't let her play until she knew what she was doing.

Good, Alex thought. They'd help her set boundaries of a new kind, based on courtesy and respect. Jake and One Bird would heal her, just as they'd healed Jaguar. She'd be fine here. He could leave her without guilt. Maybe that's why Jake kept him waiting—so he'd know that.

He made it through the day and through a quiet supper with Jake and One Bird, but when it came time to sleep, he couldn't. He tried tossing and turning for a while, then he got up and went outside to observe the stars in their infinite stillness, hoping it would help still his own anxiety. As he stood staring up at the sky, just outside the circle of houses, he heard soft steps behind him. He turned and looked.

Jake came and stood next to him. "Couldn't sleep?" he asked.

"Nope," Alex said.

"Something on your mind?"

"Something," Alex agreed. "Thought I'd come out and see if the stars could help."

"Jaguar always loved to watch the stars," Jake said. "She slept outside more than inside. Makes sense she lives up there on those Planetoids."

"It does," Alex agreed. He wouldn't push. He would wait and let the conversation develop.

"You must miss her," Jake said, "going through all this trouble to find her."

"I miss her," Alex admitted.

"And I bet she's lonely out there, under that big sky."

Alex opened his mouth, then shut it again. So she was in the area. Under that big sky. Jake sent her to walk the mesas maybe. Get her vision straight.

"Maybe not. She didn't want me to come along," Alex said truthfully.

"But you got here anyway."

Alex grinned. "Yes, I did."

Jake rocked back and forth on his heels and gazed up, away toward the jagged edge of mountains. "Had a funny dream last night," he noted.

"Good night for it," Alex said. "Full moon."

"That's right. Jaguar moon. That's what I dreamt about. Funny."

"Funny," Alex echoed.

"The moon was way up in the sky, then it fell down and down to earth. Landed west of here about 30 miles, way up on a mesa. Place where the snake lives. Place where the rainbow visits."

"Sundagger?" Alex asked.

"Just left of there. The next one over. And when it landed, it turned into a big cat. The cat looks up and lets out one of them cat howls, but nobody answers."

"Why's she howling?"

"Some guy's got her tail in a trap. Trying to hold her down."

"That's not very nice."

"Not very smart, either."

They were silent for a long time. Jake spit into the dust, sang a tuneless chant.

"Jaguar's mother saw visions," he said at last. "That's why she left the village, following a man. Some people said he had yellow eyes, like a cat. Some said he was a Spaniard. She followed him for a week. When she came back, she was pregnant. Most people thought he was a spirit man. Cougar man, they called him. She wouldn't say. Then she had Jaguar. Then she died."

Alex made no comment. This was Jaguar's story as Jake saw it. All he had to do was listen.

"When Jaguar was little she started like her mother. Dreams. Visions. Her grandfather taught her to be careful. Not get carried off like her mother did. But she was stubborn. When she came back from Manhattan, she was even more stubborn. She went off to the mesa to be one of the sun people. They don't have children. She won't have children."

Jake turned toward him. "To some people, that makes a difference."

"Not to me."

Jake was quiet. He looked at the sky. He looked at the ground. He considered his hands. "Jaguar—she's not the kind of woman who takes help easy," he said flatly. "She might bite."

"I know that about her," Alex replied. "And that doesn't matter either."

"Good," Jake said. "That's good"

He held out his hand, opened it. Cupped in his palm was something small and dark. Alex stared at it until it assumed coherent shape. It was black and shiny. Obsidian, intricately carved in the aspect of a face that was half cat and half wolf, threaded onto a leather thong.

"Her grandfather made it when she was born," Jake said. "Gave it to me when he went to New York. He said I'd know who it belonged to, when the time came. You think you want it?"

"I know I do," Alex replied.

"Then it's yours."

Alex took it, put it around his neck and tied it at the back. The carving was smooth and cool against the skin at his throat.

"There's some things you should bring with you," Jake said. "Some things you should know. I'll get what you need and—hey—how about a beer before you leave?"

* * * *

When the stars were moving through the night toward morning Alex took the airrunner and headed out, circling the canyon, looking for the best place to put it down. Jake said the mesa next to Sundagger, so he chose a mesa one over as his stopping place. From there, when the sun rose he could find her visually, see what she was up to before he approached. He was grateful for the almost silent engine of this vehicle, glad the night was clear enough to forgo using its large headlights. He'd rather his arrival was a surprise.

As he got out and looked around he already felt her presence, but couldn't yet pick her out as distinguished from the land. She'd become a part of it, the beating of her heart joined with the pulse of the planet. But she was here, and she was alive. That much he knew, and that was enough for now.

He scanned his landing spot. Here, the bones of the earth were laid bare and available for consultation. Layers of birth were recorded here, movement carved in time. The rocks had eyes and each one housed a spirit. He checked in with them.

All friendly, as far as he could tell. Perhaps they would help.

He found shelter under the dome arch of rock carved by wind and water. He could see well from here. A good view of the mesa next to him. He knew she wasn't there yet, but the land was so quiet, he thought that when she arrived he should be able to pick up her pulse on a bet.

He settled in to listen to the wind's story and wait for her to show.

* * * *

Jaguar watched the sun pull itself up over the horizon, then climbed slowly toward the sky.

She walked to a rock where a bowl had been carefully carved out for offerings, prayers.

She splashed water from her bottle into it. Sprinkled mint on it. Said the morning blessing.

Then she sat, the sun to her right, facing north. Where her enemy lived.

The sparse arid lands stretched out before her. The clarity of this place, the absolute absence of clutter, should make it easy for Senci to find her, now that she'd called him.

Or so she hoped. On the other hand, she might be difficult of apprehension. She'd become like this land, honed to bare necessities. Clean and narrow as flame. She would blend in with her surroundings. And she was about to be refined even further as she sat on the rocks and let the sun find her. A dry sweat, to burn herself clean of any extraneous matter.

The sun climbed its way into the sky, pressing itself against her back, fiery hands stroking her, rubbing at her skin. She let it burn all superfluity away, leaving nothing in her heart except her work and her death.

She lay back on the rock and stared up. What else was left to let go of? What else did she regret leaving behind? The answer came swiftly, with the heat of the sun.

Alex.

She saw his eyes. The sweet pleasure of his eyes. She pushed a hand skyward, pressing him away.

"No," she said. He was one of the remaining thoughts to burn away. She rolled over and stretched herself across the rock, belly to stone, as if it were her lover. She pressed her face into its rough surface, her lips against it, her tongue licking its dry bones. The earth pulsed against her groin in the rhythms of lovemaking, more intense than any she'd known with any man.

Except for Alex.

"No," she whispered again into the sandy surface of the rock. It was gritty against her skin, old and capable of absorbing even that fire. She had to cut herself from the thought of him. When Senci arrived, she must have no distractions. The sun, an old friend, would help her get rid of them.

There was a song One Bird used to sing, the story of a woman who saw a shaft of light enter her darkened room. It struck deep within her, engendering new life. She grew round and, for her part, she was happy. She was filled with life.

Soon, she gave birth to twins.

Twin sons, bursting with health.

The young woman's father was angry. He'd kept her safely locked away, walls of stone around her, and now this. His daughter, giving birth to twins. But she remained happy. She dreamed. She dreamed and dreamed of the sun.

She dreamed of him until he found her again, and their joy was so profound, their lovemaking so intense that she became the fire she loved and left her people, left her twin sons, left the earth. Now, she was a star in the southern sky.

One Bird learned that story from Jaguar's grandfather. It was part of the Mertec tradition of Sun Watchers—young women who waited for the sun at the summer solstice and seduced his return in midwinter. They were made sacred by the contact, their dreams and visions taken seriously. One Bird told her about these young women, and warned her of the dangers they faced. Easy enough to die, out in the sun all day or freezing through the winter night, and even if you didn't, what you did set you apart. Young men saw you as too powerful, as already husbanded by fire. Sun Watchers rarely married, and they didn't have children except the spirit kind.

But while telling her all the reasons not to do this, One Bird also taught her all the steps of the ritual and where to perform it. Thus, in her sixteenth year, Jaguar stole Jake's horse and rode to Sundagger on the summer solstice, stood naked and faced the sun.

What she felt and saw there was part of a vision she never revealed. It had to do with her name, and where her gift of chant shaping came from. It had to do with who she would become, and what would be asked of her in return.

One Bird was right. It set her apart. The young men of the village stepped aside when she passed. They looked at her with admiration and respect, but didn't ask her to dance. And no lover had been the same since.

Except Alex.

"That's not true," she protested. "It can't be true."

The golden face of the sun stared down at her. She felt his heat rake like nails down her back. She raised her head from the stone and looked around.

There was motion nearby.

"Snake," she said.

She waited, watched a sleek form uncoil itself and emerge from under her rock. She pulled a glass bottle from her pack, along with a forked stick carved to just the right proportions.

She brought the stick down at the back of the snake's neck, holding while it twisted and rattled and writhed. She lifted the snake and got the glass bottle under its teeth and let it bite until venom flowed. When it ran dry, she let it go.

It slithered to a different rock, found itself a different patch of shade. She saw it curled in shadow, staring at her with something like irritation at her rudeness.

"Little brother," she whispered, "thank you for your help."

She closed up the bottle and put it away. She'd milked seven snakes since she'd arrived. That was more than enough by any standards. She wouldn't be bothering them again.

* * * *

Alex didn't remember sleeping but he must have because suddenly he was wakened by a sense of Jaguar's unguarded presence. She was on the mesa, where Jake said she'd be.

He sat up fast, then stood, looking through the bright light of late morning.

She was directly across from him. He felt her there, and as he sought her he could see her form, sitting up on a rock. What was she doing? He paused, frowning, and figured it out.

Snakes, he thought. Snakes. Jake told him about her plans. He was horrified, even while he thought how elegant of her. How terrible and beautiful.

And now, here she was, carrying it out.

He grabbed his pack and walked down his mesa, then crossed the trail that led to hers. He didn't rush, knowing she wasn't going anywhere until Senci showed up. At the foot of her mesa he paused, gathered his strength, and started up. She was out of his view as he climbed, and then, miraculously, he stood in front of her, no more than a yard away from her, seeing her again.

She wasn't yet aware of him. She was lying back on a long, smooth rock, eyes closed. He let his eyes travel her length. The unbleached cloth of her ceremonial dress was lighter than her sun-burnished skin. He noticed how finely drawn she looked, as if she'd been refined in the same fires that forge steel. Everything about her was necessary and true.

And she was preparing herself to die.

"Not on my watch," he murmured.

At the sound of his voice she startled, opened her eyes, looked at him blankly. In a moment, her brain confirmed what her eyes told her and she glared at him. "Get out of here," she said through clenched teeth. "Leave. You'll get yourself killed."

In spite of her anger, she didn't shift a molecule. A rattlesnake slid up the rock, curled around her head and made its way down her belly. It stared at him as she did, and waited.

He moved to her, but not fast enough. The rattler's tail sang its song and he struck, sinking his fangs into her arm as she cursed prolifically.

"Christ," Alex said. He pulled the snake off her and flung him into the sand, where he twisted, writhed, then slithered swiftly away. Alex reached for her arm and she offered her elbow in his face as an alternative. He swung his legs over her, straddled her and wrapped his hands around her forearms as she struggled against him, twisting and arching her back.

"Stop it," she said, her voice low and breathy. "You're just making it more difficult."

"Difficult?" He shook her roughly. "Dammit, Jaguar, I *want* it to be difficult. I want it to hurt like hell. It does for me."

"You think I'm taking a walk in the park?"

"Then why didn't you tell me?"

"Because I knew you'd show. You always show. You're reliable as death. How did you find me?"

He caught her gaze, held it hard.

My eyes have always found you. You know that.

She went still, all her muscles relaxed. She closed her eyes and fell back onto the rock. He took the risk of releasing one of her arms to get at a jacknife in his pocket. She remained immobile as he cross-cut her flesh, sucked the blood and spit it into the hot sandy soil.

"You don't understand," she said to him, now cool and distant. "You can't be here. You have to let me do this alone."

"Don't," he said, between spitting and sucking, "be ridiculous."

She turned her face from him. He ripped a piece of cloth from his shirt and tore it in two—one for a bandage, and the other for a soft tourniquet. She lay still while he worked, continued passive when he pulled a water bottle from his belt holder and held it to her lips.

"Drink," he said. She regarded him as venomously as the snake.

"Drink," he insisted, and she did so, but her eyes stayed angry.

"Jaguar," he said, "What makes you think your job here necessarily includes your death?"

"It's not my death I'm worried about," she said. "It's yours."

He saw fear in her eyes and knew she had a basis for it. She wasn't an Adept, but she'd seen something that looked like his death here. And he didn't care. Not even a little bit.

He swung his leg over the rock and got off her. "Jake and One Bird didn't send you here to die. Not me, either."

She sat up, looked at him hard. Her gaze moved to the fetish he wore around his neck and she winced.

"They sent you?" she demanded. "With that?"

"They did."

"Shit," she said. "That's why Jake kept stalling. He was waiting for you."

"Was he?" Alex commented. "Smart man."

She glowered at him. "No," she said.

"I already said yes."

"You don't know what you're saying yes to."

"Oh yes I do. Jake told me about the snakes and the poison. He gave me the antidote. He said he gave it to you, but you left it behind."

"There's no point, Alex. Senci has to feed off me to get the poison, and there's no antidote for that. And if I don't go to him, he'll kill you. Then Rachel, and Gerri and—anyone I care about."

"You think I'd let that happen?"

"You think you can stop him? He always kills what I love. He's been doing it since I was a little girl."

At her words, Alex went still. "What are you talking about?"

She ducked her head down, said nothing.

"Jaguar, tell me," he demanded.

She lifted her face, pressed her hand to his forehead and showed him.

She was a little girl and a man stood over her, holding a gun. He took her clothes off and his hands, encased in gloves, moved over her.

Alex knew this scene. She'd shown it to him when they were first learning to trust each other. Just after she saved his life. Why was she showing it to him now?

Jaguar's voice spoke into his confusion.

Look at his eyes, Alex. It's the only thing he hasn't changed.

Once again Alex viewed the scene, and though in the past he'd always seen it from the point of view of the little girl who'd become this woman he valued so deeply, this time he shifted his focus and saw her attacker's eyes. In his shock, he broke empathic contact.

"Jesus," he said out loud. "It was Senci."

Senci, the Greenkeeper. The man who raped her. The ghost who would never die, finding her again.

"I'm bound to him," Jaguar said quietly. "He's a Greenkeeper and he bound me when—when he did that to me. Now he'll kill everyone I love. And there's no antidote for that, either."

Through the pulsing of his own rage and her pain, Alex groped for something that would help. All he found was one singular truth. Something he knew beyond reason or doubt.

"No," he said firmly. "You're tied to him by circumstance, but he didn't bind you to him. Not as a Greenkeeper does." He rested his hand on her arm, where the snake had bitten her. "Where do you get the antidote for snake bite?" he asked her.

"From the snake, of course. Turn poison into medicine. What's that got to do with—"

"That's what you do, Jaguar. It's what you've always done. You take the poison of your life and turn it into medicine. You wouldn't do that if you were his. Don't you see? He *can't* bind you. That's why he's obsessed with having you now."

She eyed him suspiciously. "You don't know that," she said.

"I do, but you don't. Not yet. That's the problem." He ran a hand through his hair. His words wouldn't convince her. She'd have to find this one her own way. In the meantime, he had to keep her alive. "Look, no matter what, Jake and One Bird sent me here to partner the warrior in her task. I plan on doing just that."

She closed her eyes. A fly landed on her hand, and she twitched it away. They were silent, listening to the singing wind.

"That's what you want?" she asked at last.

"That's exactly what I'll do," he said.

"Alex, when Senci finds me I'll inject myself with enough venom to kill a horse, then let him feed. The only thing left after that is to cut his heart out, get it to the choc mul and say the cleansing prayer. If I can't, that'll be your job. Can you do it?"

He struggled with words, came up with something reasonable. "I'll do what's necessary," he said. "That's why I'm here."

"Are you sure?"

"Yes. I'm here because I'm sure."

Another pause. Then, "There's a ceremony," she said. "When you partner the warrior, there's a ceremony."

"Jake told me."

She nodded. "We should do it tonight. I'm not sure when he'll show up."

He touched the place where the rattler bit her. "Are you up to it?"

She waved it away. "I milked that one twice before he bit me. He had nothing left."

Of course, he thought. Of course. She'd fling herself off a cliff, but she wouldn't be pushed.

She pulled herself to standing, rubbed her face with her hand, felt her lips, which were still not hydrated. Alex, seeing the gesture, handed her the water bottle, and she drank. When she handed it back to him, he folded his hand over hers.

It felt good to be in her presence again. In spite of fear and the near presence of death, to be here with her was good and he was glad of it.

As often happened, her words echoed his thoughts. "I know I shouldn't say this," she said, "But I'm glad you're here. "

He touched a finger to her face. She closed her eyes and leaned into it briefly. Yes, he thought. We are here. All this, and still I'm courting her, and she's glad of it.

She opened her eyes, and shifted attitude back to the business at hand.

"Okay," she said. "The ceremony's a night one, but we should head up higher before dark. There's a place, and it takes a while to get there."

CHAPTER 19

AS THEY CLIMBED THE MESA the earth spread out below them, red rock shifting in the growing darkness to gold, tan, brown. There were ripples in the sandstone where the tide once rose and fell. Though they walked the stone bones of earth, all around them was the sense of ancient seas.

Jaguar, stopping to rest, swept a long arm across the mesa. "I used to be afraid of these climbs," she noted.

"You?"

"Mm. When I was a teenager. I was a city kid for almost ten years, and I forgot what it was like here. I trusted buildings, but not my feet. "

"What changed?"

"Jake reminded me how to let the stones hold my feet. How to trust them. Now I'm not so sure about buildings." She put down her backpack and rubbed at her neck. "That was a long time ago," she said.

Alex noted again how the land was reflected in her face. How she was, like this place, honed down to her singular and particular being. He pulled his eyes away from her and looked up.

Above them, the rock turned white and softly luminescent. Grottoes were carved out, little temples, of a size for two people to shelter in.

Jaguar pointed to them. "There," she said.

They walked on soft sand, fine as pulverized silk, toward the pouched wall of rock. Jaguar dropped her pack at the edge of it and indicated that Alex should do the same. He reached into his pack and pulled out two robes made of soft linen, the color of wheat with black and red figures dancing here and there. "Jake said we'd want these."

She held her hand out for one of the robes. "All ritual is just another fashion opportunity," she smiled grimly. "My people are big on style, in case you didn't notice."

"I noticed. Years ago."

She sighed. "Okay. Change. Get ready. When Venus is up, come back here."

* * * *

They were sheltered in the bones of the earth, in a place where the sky was bigger than his ability to imagine it. Against a wall of stone was a very old choc mul, a bowl held on the belly of a man who waited for the sacrificial heart. Nearby Jaguar had arranged a long and intricately carved stick, a small pouch, and a piece of sharp obsidian.

"Here," she said, and invited him to sit. She walked around him, drawing a circle in the sand with the stick. When she was done she sat down facing him and sang softly, a chant he hadn't heard before. It went on and on, weaving into the night and him, weaving him into the sky and stones, weaving her into him and all that lived here.

The candle she lit threw shadows up the rock, washed their white curves with darkness. His shadow was a great bird. She, standing with arms upraised, was a shadow moon over his shadow bird.

Time slowed as they entered that liminal space they both knew, wandering in a world made of no words. He felt his own body slowing, going quiet, going into truth. There were stars here, silent and watchful. And there was Jaguar, a focused light through which truth could flow.

She would have to know him essentially if she was to accept his partnership. He would have to be unafraid for that to happen. Her voice poured over them both, water in the dry places. The candle flickered and caused their shadows to dance and leap toward each other.

Her song ceased before he ceased hearing it, the sound echoing through him as background to what followed as she raised two fingers to his heart and established the space they would share.

Who are you? she asked, initiating the questions.

Alex Dzarny.

Show me, her voice asked, opening him.

For this, there were no words. She rode his spirit with him, made of earth, its molten core burning slow and sure. Reliable as death. Solid as the stone that witnessed this ceremony. A spirit who danced fearlessly with time, aware of its complexity in a way few others were. This was a place she hadn't traversed before, a place he was glad enough to show her.

Who shares soul with you?

The spirit that fed him his energy, shared a portion of his soul. He offered her the image of a wolf, standing atop a mountain and howling to a glowing moon. A creature that stood high and saw far, a pathfinder that gave him his capacities as an Adept.

She allowed it, and moved on.

Who chooses you?

That. The spirit who stalked him, demanded his attention, taught him what he might not want to know. A story he hadn't yet told her. He did so now, offering his earliest and most persistent vision.

In a dream, he walked through a rainforest, toward a river. There, in the river, a golden jaguar floated, beckoning him.

I choose you, she said. I choose you.

He showed Jaguar this and she halted her singing, caught for a moment between her role in the ceremony and her more human self. She mastered herself and moved on. The ceremony swirled around them, returning them to quiet. She searched under his memory for any untruth, walking through him easily and thoroughly.

Why are you here? she asked.

To partner the warrior.

Why do you choose this?

He hesitated. There were so many answers he could give, and only one mattered here. He took a deep breath and spoke it.

Because I love you, Jaguar. I always have and always will. Always.

Silence. She closed her eyes and let the words rest between them, tasting their truth. She moved through his experience of them, absorbing it into her own soul, feeling everything it meant to him. Did she find his words sweet, he wondered? They were to him. Sweet to say, after all this silence.

She began the concluding chant and grasped his hand. Sharp stone bit into his flesh. Obsidian, hidden in her hand, drawing his blood. He didn't flinch. She brought her lips to the wound and drank. They were partnered, for good or ill.

Words followed. Elaborate praise for ancestors and spirits that her people had known for thousands of generations. It went on for some time, carrying them into realms Alex always suspected lived in the worlds behind her eyes.

Then, an ending.

"There will be no lies between or within us," she said. "We live and die with our task, start and finish in beauty. Long life. Honey in the heart. No evil. 13 thank yous."

He repeated the words, and she led him to the choc mul, let blood drip from his hand into the bowl. And it was done.

She walked over the circle she'd traced in the sand, wiping it out with her foot. When she finished, she walked away, not looking back. He opened his hand and gazed down at the wound, already closing. His blood belonged to her now.

But he already knew that.

* * * *

As soon as he knew she was far enough away not to be spying he went to work, and he worked fast, knowing what he had to do.

He went through her pack, muttering at her under his breath about recklessness and folly. He would be her partner in the truest sense, looking out for her well being when she could not. He found her glass bottle of venom, did what was necessary, then put all back as it had been.

When he finished, he thought through his moves. He had a gun with the right kind of bullets, and though it wouldn't kill Senci, it could buy them the seconds they needed. It could work.

And if it didn't? They'd both be dead, he supposed.

If, he thought, and if and if. That was what he had, and no matter how many times he thought it through, that's all he was going to get for now. He stood and left the shelter of the stones.

* * * *

When he walked out of the grotto the night was as deep as it would get, and the immensity of stars overhead was a reeling of all time imaginable. Jaguar stood still and attentive at the rim of the mesa, looking out over the canyon. He walked toward her, then stopped a few yards back.

"Jaguar," he said.

She whirled to face him, a long finger extended toward him. "I've *never* said I love you."

He smiled. Here she was on the edge of doom, worrying this small problem like a bad tooth. Good for her for focusing on what mattered. Good for him, in many ways. Then, the words of the ceremony echoed in his mind. There will be no lies between us.

"Deny it," he said.

She opened her mouth, closed it again.

"Go ahead, Jaguar," he coaxed. "Tell me you don't love me."

Her lips moved, seeking the right words, knowing the ones she couldn't say, unwilling to say the only truth she was allowed to speak. "Alex," she said desperately. "I came here to die. How can I do that if I love you?"

"Love beats death every time," he replied. "You of all people know that."

She held her hands out, pleading. "It hurts. *Don't* make me love you."

"I don't have to," he said, coming up to her and catching hold of her hands. "It's already done."

He pulled her close and a moan rose from the back of her throat, perhaps the back of her skull. Then his mouth was on hers and she moved against him, and he thought he'd go mad with joy.

Say it, Jaguar.

She groped for his hand, pressed it against her heart so he could feel it beating hard against his skin.

I have never loved any man except you, except you Alex I love you.

He kept his hand on her heart, wanting what lived there. He would do this in empathic contact. Wanted to make love to her that way. With full intent. At full risk.

This way, he said. *All of you and all of me.*
Now, Alex?
Now is what we have.

Now. Now. All or nothing, here in the land where everything was necessary. He'd never tried it before, and from what she'd told him neither had she. They didn't know what would happen. But at least here, if they achieved critical mass, nobody would be hurt. And the stones would remember them. The wind would sing their song.

She let herself wash into him and he joined her at the place where he was only Alex and she was only Jaguar. They washed into each other, sweet as evening. Sweet as cool sleep and waking in sun. He felt her shiver of pleasure as she felt his, and both felt the spark of what it meant to the other. They became fire feeding fire, the fury of her passion a song he sang back to her here in this deep place, hidden and nurtured like wild strawberries growing under long grass. His hands ran over her breasts, her belly, down her hips and the back of her thighs. She bit at his face, the side of his neck, biting and kissing with a hunger long denied.

They dropped their robes onto the sandy soil and became no more than the animals they shared soul with, who danced with them here, elegantly, on the mesa.

* * * *

This is how her skin tasted to him. Like wild strawberries that disappear on the tongue and smell of stars.

And her lips, soft and smooth under his, and her thighs pressing against him, her mouth, sliding across his shoulder, tasting like wild strawberries on the tongue. This is where they met each other, sweet and sure, direct as stars. He tasted and fed her the longing that lived in his mouth, and she drank it and gave him back what poured down her throat.

You taste like stars, he whispered into her.

This is how he touched her breasts, how they felt in his mouth and how she felt him tasting them.

All this? All this, Alex?
This, and more.

This is how he pulled her onto the sand under him, and pressed himself into her as her body stretched to meet him, drawing him in, tidal and sure. This the arch of her back as she tilted her hips to him. This the feel of his bones moving against her hips. This the rhythm they found with no breaks in it, rocking like thunder on the desert floor, the sky falling all around. This is how he put his fingers to her face and kept her eyes with his, how she bruised his skin with her nails, feeling his joy as it joined hers, which he absorbed like a morning of first stars.

Jaguar, here. This. Like this.
Yes. This. At last.
This.

This is how he gave her the sky, the epicenter of the quake, the place where he could break like glass. This is how she swam within it, and how he felt her delicate motion. This her lightning coursing the pathways of his nerves and how she knew his joy at its song. This his howl into the night of her mouth and why he must go deeper always deeper to find her again and again and feel her witness what his discovery meant to him.

Here. I give you this, Jaguar. All the gods know it's always been yours.

This is the gift he gave her, as he found her and let himself be found. This is the gift she gave him, drawing him in to where depth and breadth became moot measures because all was depth, all was breadth.

And their eyes, seeing the universe in each other and themselves.

And the names they called to the arid night, the divine arms that wrapped them.

Jaguar, he cried into the sea of her that he knew like his own heart.

Alex, she called to the earth he was made of that she lived within.

* * * *

When the stars had set and the sky in the east began to go silver, her eyes were still open, looking at him without cover or defense.

"How do you feel?" she asked.

"I feel everything," he answered. "All at once, without exception. You?

"Honey in the heart," she said.

"Honey in the heart," he repeated. He kissed her and found she tasted no less sweet at dawn than she had at midnight. A good sign, he thought.

"You are so beautiful," he murmured, "So beautiful, Jaguar."

"Hush," she said. "There's better ways to use your mouth than flattery."

He laughed, and complied.

CHAPTER 20

JAKE WOKE IN THE EARLY MORNING LIGHT to something that sounded like a squealing pig. He was old, maybe forgot a few things now and then, but he knew they didn't have any pigs on the premises.

He swung his legs out of bed and found that One Bird was, as usual, just a little ahead of him, pushing herself into a housedress.

"What is it?" Jake asked.

"It's the girl," she told him. She looked out the window. "I think—Red Feather's got her. She's kicking hard, though." She chuckled in approval.

They exited the house, and when Maya saw them, she went from squealing to screeching.

"Tell him to let me *go*," she screeched. "I have to go *lemme go!*"

"Hold on," Jake said, and walked over to them. He put a hand on Red Feather's shoulder. "It's okay. We'll take it from here."

"She's a little crazy. You know that," Red Feather observed.

"That's okay," One Bird said. "He likes his women that way."

Red Feather grinned and loosened his hold. Maya slid from his arms to the ground, picked herself up, and took off at a run.

"Hey," Jake yelled. "I'm too old to chase you."

She looked back, stumbled and fell. Then she sat in the dust, lowering her head into her hands. Jake and One Bird walked over and squatted down next to her.

"Maybe," One Bird suggested, "you should tell us what you want. Maybe we can help."

She lowered her hands from her tear and dirt stained face. "It's Jaguar. I have to find her. She doesn't understand he's a liar."

Jake reached over and ran a finger lightly across her forehead. "You have a dream about her?"

Maya's eyes grew wide. "How do you know?"

"He's good at dreams," One Bird said. "Everybody's gotta be good at something. What did you dream?"

"She—she was up on a hill. Not a hill. Like a big flat piece of rock. He was there. And she believed him, but he's a liar and if she believes him, he'll kill her. I have to go and tell her."

Jake turned to One Bird. "What do you think?" he asked.

One Bird closed her eyes, then opened them again. "Let her go."

Jake shook his head. "We don't know a lot about her yet. Maybe she's—"

"If you already decided," One Bird said, "why'd you ask me?"

Jake pressed his hands against his knees and rose with a groan. "I'll get a car. We can drive her most of the way in, then leave her off. I suppose she can't make it any worse."

* * * *

In the later part of the morning Alex put his jeans and t-shirt back on and took the trek back to the airrunner to get more water and food, supplies in case they had to wait through another day for Senci to show. By the time he returned the sun was riding toward noon, but when he crested the top of the mesa Jaguar was nowhere to be seen.

A moment of panic gripped him. He dropped his backpack and started moving toward the grotto where they'd done the ceremony. Just before he called her name he saw her walking out from behind a stand of boulders. She still wore the ceremonial dress of the night before, which created the strange perception that she was a living stone painted in glyphs, moving to him.

"Jesus," he said, when she was close enough to hear him. "Don't scare me that way."

"I had to pee, Alex," she replied. "Did you want to watch?"

"I—what is it, Jaguar?"

"He's getting closer. I can feel him."

Alex was aware of his heart pounding, equally aware of her shift into high tension.

"Jaguar, there's still time. We can get to the airrunner, take it back to Jake's or head out for a shuttle."

Her face showed compassion. "You know we can't. And you know what you have to do. You made a promise."

He opened his mouth to argue then stopped himself. "I'll do what's right," he said carefully. "Just sit next to me. Let's go into this quietly."

She folded herself on the ground next to him and he held onto her hands. They were cold. He gathered what strength he had and put it into them for her.

"You can't back out," she said. "It's not just me. You know what he is. What he can do. All the children he could take—what I might do if he takes me. Alex, this is too important not to get it right."

"Did I say I'd partner you? I won't let him do any of that."

"Okay. I—okay. Listen, there's something else. Make sure—my body—" she paused.

This was too much, he thought. Too much for either of them.

"Get it back to Jake and One Bird. They'll know what to do," she concluded.

"Don't talk. Rest a minute. One minute more is ours."

"I shouldn't have let you love me. Shouldn't have let myself—"

"Like I said. Love beats death every time. Let it, Jaguar. Just let it."

She slowed her breathing and rested her hands in his, allowing him to give her this gift of one moment. One moment more between them. Her eyes, sea green and gold as the earth, held his, and he let them. Let her hold on for as long as she wants, he thought. For as long as she wants she can hold me. Forever.

Her head jerked back and she stared past him, out onto the canyon floor. "He's here," she said. "You have to go. Over there in the rocks." She pointed to a stand of boulders about 15 feet away.

"Jaguar—"

"*Go*," she snapped. "Now."

No time left to tell her, to talk her into it. He'd have to play it out, and hope she caught up. She usually did. He moved quickly to the rocks, and soon was invisible among them.

CHAPTER 21

SHE STOOD VERY STILL, HER BACK TO THE SUN. Senci appeared on the other side of the mesa and began to walk toward her across the broad expanse of smooth white stone and scattered sage, past the place where Alex crouched behind boulders. Closer. He was getting closer.

"So," she said. "Here we are at last."

At last. At last.

Senci curved a hand out and she felt herself pulled to him. He was sure of himself now. Sure of her.

She allowed herself to be pulled. She needed to get close. He turned his eyes to her, eyes that ached with nothing. Nothing. Like old hands on her flesh.

How many years had he done this? How many years, so that life and death were the same to him, death his only concern because he would not die. What would it be like to be fucked by walking death?

Cold. The closer he drew, the colder she felt

When she was a child and he raped her, she'd gone numb quickly. He wouldn't let her escape that way now. Instinctively, she took a step back.

His hand balled into a fist. A surge of pain coursed through her. He pulled her to him while she struggled to be still and let him.

Come to me, my Jaguar.

Nightmare. This was the nightmare part. Waves of sucking death drawing her close. She remembered the feel of it from when she was a child. But in her hand she held the means to end the nightmare. A hypodermic filled with venom, the gift of the snakes. He reached for her, draining her strength and carrying her to him. To him. Only a few more steps and he could touch her. The smell of something burning was all around. With effort, she kept hold of the needle. The wind moaned through her, around her, in her.

His face twisted in pleasure at her pain. He was feeding from it. Feeding already. Close enough to touch her now, and he was savoring the moment. A voice emerged from his coldness.

I will hold you to me. You will be bound to me forever.

No, she thought, I won't.

Greenkeepers bound through energy, primarily the energy of fear, and in spite of everything she wasn't afraid. Love beats death every time, Alex said. And it beats fear even worse. She did not fear him. She had the means of her own escape. He had no power over her.

No power.

That. It was important. She held herself back, took a moment to understand. That thought, it was important. It reminded her of something

Jake told her, of something Alex said about why Senci chased her, why he needed her. She let it fall into place and at last, she understood, not with her mind but with her heart. A moment of luminous clarity filled her, and she spoke it.

"You couldn't bind me," she said with something like wonder. "You're here *because* you couldn't. Because you never could and never will."

He smiled, but she saw the muscle twitching at his jaw.

"I wasn't afraid of you, and I'm still not," she said. "I knew you'd never have me, that I was better than you. And that's why you want me."

Of course. That was it. He could beat death, but he still feared it. She couldn't beat death, but the fear of it didn't rule her. Her victory was greater, and he wanted to eat it, make it his own.

"You're the one who's bound," she whispered.

His eyes went dark with rage and he took two steps closer until she could smell the poison of his breath.

I will feed off you. Have what you have. Make it mine.

Now, she told herself. Do it now.

"Love beats death every time," she muttered, and she jammed the hypo into her thigh. Soon she'd be dead. Just time enough for him to feed, and Alex would take care of the rest. She could count on him, reliable as death.

She waited to feel the first shock of poison enter her, the burning and dizziness and sharp pain.

Nothing happened.

She felt nothing. No poison. Nothing. She looked at the hypodermic cupped inside her hand. No poison filled her.

"Alex," she whispered. "You didn't."

Of course I did.

His answer reverberated across the mesa, speaking into her. Of course he did. She should have known he would. Her hypo was filled with water, not venom. He wouldn't let her do this. But what did he have as an alternative?

Looking over Senci's shoulder, she saw him approaching, a C21 cobalt fire weapon in his hand, filled with toxic bullets. Only that? She pressed a finger against her wrist to release the glass blade of her knife. If that's how he felt, she'd fight it out with him to the end.

Then, someone screamed.

A high-pitched chain of sound rolled over them, the kind only a little girl could produce. They all turned toward it. Maya was hurtling at them, screaming as she came.

She flung herself at Senci and attached herself to his arm, biting, kicking and screaming. Jaguar tried to pull her off like a tick or a cat whose claws were stuck. Alex raised his weapon and fired at Senci again and again.

Senci raised a hand and stopped the bullets before they could hit. Alex, running toward them, kept firing until Senci flicked a wrist and Alex's weapon flew out, landed in the dust. Quick as thought Senci back-handed Maya and she lay stunned in the dust. He twisted his face down to her, smiling.

It would take him less than a second to fling her off the mesa, only seconds more to do the same with Alex. Jaguar would not let him. Not this time.

As Alex raced toward them she raised her knife, aimed it at Senci's heart and lunged.

Senci laughed.

Senci laughed and moved his hand, a casual gesture. Moved his hand and pulled Alex between them, just as Jaguar's knife came down.

Her knife, meant for Senci, fell into Alex's chest. His eyes were unsurprised, clear and glinting with some unfathomable victory as her blade entered him.

Her nightmare, inescapable. And Senci laughed.

Jaguar tried to pull back but Alex swayed and leaned into her, pushing the knife further in.

No No Alex No.

Senci laughed.

Alex grabbed Jaguar's wrist and held hard. They stood very close, her knife in his chest, his eyes triumphant. He put a hand on her shoulder and fell to his knees, bringing her with him down to the warm, soft earth.

Jaguar.

Her lips moved, but no sound emerged. Her hand was slippery with his blood and water fell suddenly from her eyes. Her worst nightmare. No words. Nothing but horror and tears falling as if she couldn't stop them ever again. Her deepest grief here, inescapable.

Alex released her hand and she pulled her knife from him, horrified at the feel of it, the sound of it. He moved his bloodied hand to her face, taking her tears as he gave her his blood.

Senci stood behind her and laughed.

Alex leaned heavily on her shoulder and pushed himself up to his feet. He offered his hand to Senci, who bared his teeth at it.

"Blood," Alex said, his voice a whisper. "My blood. Hungry?"

Jaguar tried to rise but Alex held her where she was. Senci grabbed Alex's hand and licked at it. Licked and swallowed hungrily, then stopped.

Everything in him stopped. His face twisted in pain and he clutched at his mouth, full of Alex's blood and Jaguar's tears.

Alex laughed.

"What's wrong?" he asked. "Too much salt?"

He released Jaguar, staggered forward and pressed his bloodied hand onto Senci's forehead. Jaguar's tears sizzled against his skin. Alex began to shake all over.

Everything he was he showed to Senci. All his profound courtesy. His willingness to be here, dying so Jaguar could live. The absence of fear in his dying, like hers. Like hers. He gave it all to Senci, whose face and mouth and throat burned with her tears. And in the mirror of Alex's life, Senci saw what he had chased Jaguar to learn.

If he did not fear death, he could die, and in dying be transformed.

At last. At last. You have found me.

Senci fell to his knees and Alex swayed, clutching his own chest, his face blanched as blood poured from him. He bowed his head, then collapsed in on himself, his last energy spent.

Maya screamed and the ping of cobalt fire brushed past Jaguar. She fell back, scrambled to stand. The girl had Alex's gun and was firing it, her face a scream that kept happening. She fired again and again and Senci, distracted by pain, reeled back as one shot hit and made a hole in his head. He put his hand to it, trying to put it back together. Venom entered him and he writhed under its sway.

Jaguar heard Alex speaking within her.

His heart. Take his heart. For fuck's sake, do it now.

Tears still running down her face, Jaguar turned to Senci, who knelt before her with his hands at his skull. In his long life, he'd spread death and fear and pain until he'd become nothing but that. And she would release him from that burden.

She plunged her knife into his chest, slashing clean through skin and muscle and bone. She pushed her hands into him and found his heart, still beating. She closed her hand around it and pulled hard, slashing away all connective tissue until it was freed from his body. Then she held it high, singing the song One Bird taught her for the end of bondage.

I release you I release you I release you

His terror oozed onto the ground, sizzled in the air, his eyes wide and staring at sky nothing.

I release you I release you I release you I release you.

He crumbled at her feet, his body steaming red and writhing. She held his heart like a torch and ran for the grotto, where she dropped her burden into the bowl of the choc mul.

"Eat this and not me," she whispered as she laid it down.

She felt motion in the stones around her, motion in the air. Senci's spirit, making its last bid for supremacy. She backed out of the grotto, turned and ran. The earth shook under her feet and she lurched, landed on her face. She scrambled back up, moved across the trembling ground to Alex. To Alex. She would be with him while the world fell apart. While the ground shook and Senci found his way into death.

She stumbled to where Alex lay, his eyes closed now, his face quiet in the storm. She would be with him.

The day darkened to grey. The air grew hot and twisted as Senci's body swelled, eyeless and lipless and dessicated of flesh. He grew to bursting, then collapsed in on himself, a thousand years of hunger eating hunger, drawing all available air into it, drawing breath from Jaguar's body until she felt she was being turned inside out.

Don't you know love beats death every time, Jaguar?

Her lungs wouldn't work, and breath was sucked out of her by Senci's departing laughter as it screamed across the high mesa in the wind.

CHAPTER 22

<small>TIME PASSED WITHOUT BREATH FOR A MINUTE MORE THAN ETERNITY.</small>
Then her lungs worked for her, pulling in air, the clean wind of the mesa flowing into her effortlessly. She opened her eyes and saw only sky.

She was on her back on the mesa. There was something else she had to do. Something.

She pulled herself up and looked around. Alex lay next to her on a patch of earth that was too red. Maya squatted near him, weeping. A few feet away was Senci—or what was left of him. Only the thin and dusty outline of a skeleton.

As she stared at it she noticed her right hand was tightly closed. She opened it, saw she held a single leaf of mint, perfectly green and fresh as if she'd just picked it, still wet from what felt like early morning dew. Something she was supposed to do here. Yes. Of course. What One Bird and Jake told her to do.

She stood and lifted the mint to the sky, said the cleansing prayer.

She walked to where Senci had fallen and dropped the mint onto the outline of his skeleton, drawn in dust on the mesa. It came to rest where his heart had been, something green and fresh to replace an ancient evil.

The wind picked up dust and leaf, swirled it into the air and carried it to a place where stone and water would absorb it, disperse it, transform it into something it had never been before.

She took a deep breath as it passed, then went and crouched next to Alex, near Maya who wept over him. She touched his forehead. Cool and clammy. She moved her finger across his temple, down to his neck.

There, under her finger, a pulse beat. Under his skin, his heart was beating.

A sob of relief was torn from her. She ripped his shirt open and saw that the wound she'd made was high and to the left. Too far left for his heart. Too high for his lungs. Just a lot of blood vessels, muscle, and flesh, making a mess. She found his water bottle and washed the blood away, cut pieces of her dress for bandages, wrapped his wound and washed his face, put water to his lips. Kissed him.

As she did so, she felt a hand on her shoulder. She turned to Maya's ashen aspect.

"Is he dead?" Maya asked.

"No," Jaguar reassured her. "He's just unconscious. Were you hurt?"

Maya shook her head. "You fell down and I couldn't wake you up, so I sat next to him. I sang a song to him, but he didn't move. Are you sure he's not dead?"

"Put your hand by his mouth and you'll feel him breathing."

Maya's small fingers wandered to his lips and touched them tentatively, then pulled back. "I want to go to the village," she said.

Jaguar frowned. "I don't want to move him yet. When he wakes up, we'll take the airrunner."

"I think they'll be waiting for me by the road. It's only a few miles. I ran all the way here and I wasn't even tired."

"It's a long walk if they're not there. "

"I promised I'd be back for supper. Jake'll be mad if I'm not."

Jaguar smiled. Already, she was learning. Keep your promises. "You were very brave, Maya," she said. "You saved our lives."

She kicked at the dirt. "I should go," she said.

"Go on, then. Tell them what happened. Tell them we're okay."

Maya looked at her gratefully, then skittered away over the mesa. Jaguar turned back to Alex, stroked his head and sang into his dreams, softly so as not to wake him.

CHAPTER 23

THERE WERE SO MANY STARS AROUND HIM, and space was so vast. Too vast to tell what direction he floated in or how he moved. He only knew the sensation of motion as he took his spirit journey through the open universe.

Death wasn't so bad after all, Alex thought. It was, at least, beautiful. But he wished he could tell Jaguar about it. Instinctively he turned, looking for her.

And she was there.

Her face, inches from his, on sandy earth.

Had she died with him? As he tried to figure this out, he felt a tickle and reached his hand up to brush it away. Sand flea on his face.

His face?

Apparently, he still had a face. He sought out other body parts. His toes wiggled when he told them to. His legs moved. His arms—he shifted himself up on his elbow and felt pain throbbing in his shoulder. When he looked at it, saw it was actually there, he also saw it was bandaged with something that looked like Jaguar's clothes.

He had survived. Had she?

He breathed in deeply, willing his heart to slow its rapid rhythms. Then he let his fingers run lightly over the skin of her face. It felt warm to the touch. Warm and alive.

He moved two fingers to her forehead and asked permission to enter her dreams.

The shock of pleasure almost knocked him flat again. There. Jaguar's sweet jungle and she was waiting for him. He saw himself in her dream, approaching her.

"Jaguar," he said, "it's me."

She opened her eyes, stared at him hard as dream flowed into waking in this land of desert visions. She didn't ask if he was alive. She knew.

She pressed her hands to his face and he kissed her, long and slow, taking her lips as a blessing.

Look how close the stars are tonight, he said into her.

Take me there, she said. *With you.*

And he did.

EPILOGUE

THEY LINGERED FOR ANOTHER DAY AND NIGHT on the mesa, both of them reluctant to leave a place that held such blessings. There was food and water in Alex's airrunner, and they had each other, which was more than enough.

But as the second dawn rose over them, Jaguar looked to Alex and sighed. "They'll be worrying about us," she said.

"They will," he agreed. "You ready to go back?"

"More or less," she said.

They took the airrunner back to the village. Jake and One Bird, along with Maya and her new family, greeted them when they arrived, made them eat food and sleep. Jaguar called Rachel to let her know they were alive and would be staying in New Mexico a while. Rachel didn't ask what happened, or what would happen next. She just said it was good to hear her sounding like herself again.

Nobody talked about Senci or what happened on the mesa. Probably they already knew but felt it wasn't time to tell the story yet. At the sun ceremony next year was time enough. Jaguar would be asked to tell it then. And by then, she might know how.

Jaguar and Alex were quiet together. They had little to say that needed words. She was alive. He was alive. They were here with each other, in this place of singing wind. In this place where everything sings.

At One Bird's insistence they stayed a full week, letting her work her magic on Alex's shoulder. He and Jaguar walked with Maya at night, telling her the names of the stars. She regarded them with solemn eyes, always walking a little distance apart. Once, when they were admiring Jupiter and holding hands, she asked, "Why do you do that?"

"Do what?" Alex asked.

"Hold hands." She turned to Alex. "Are you afraid she'll get away?"

Jaguar elbowed Alex's ribs before he laughed. "I can get away any time I want. See?" She released his hand, took it back. "But I don't want to. I like it here."

When they walked back to the house Maya got between them and took a hand from each. She walked about five steps that way, then let them go and skipped ahead. Then she walked back and grabbed their hands again. She did this once, twice, three times. One Bird, watching from the front door of her house, nodded approval.

"Maybe," Alex suggested, "we should stay a little more and see what else we can do."

Their one week turned into two, and then three. Finally the rains came and everyone stood under them to taste the blessing. Corn was harvested and baked in pits around the houses. Every night, Alex slept with Jaguar either in her room or under the wide night sky. Every day they'd work in the gardens or play with Maya or walk the land.

Then one morning Alex found Jaguar standing outside the adobe house, staring up at the sky in the direction of the Planetoid. On a clear day, in spite of the cloaking screens, you could still make out the rim of it as a shining ring in the sky.

"Homesick?" Alex asked.

She jumped, and then turned to him. "You're the only man who can actually sneak up on me. Did you know that?"

"I think I got that figured by now. You're ready to go back, aren't you?"

She nodded. "If I don't, then I won't. This land gets under your skin, Alex. You have no idea."

"I'm beginning to figure that one, too. We better see if we can get our jobs back, first."

"Is there a problem with that?"

"You resigned, Jaguar. So did I."

"Oh," she said. "That."

"That," Alex agreed. "I'll call Paul."

Once he had Paul on the line, Alex told him that Dr. Addams and Supervisor Dzarny were alive, relatively unscathed, and ready to return to Planetoid 3.

"Huh," Paul said. "Ain't that something. You think maybe you can get jobs here?"

"Maybe. Are you upset about something, Paul?" he asked.

"Upset? Upset? You left me short all this time and we've got five new ones this week. Yes, goddammit. I'm upset. You can't just resign every time you need to chase after that crazy woman on some other...."

His words trailed to silence. Alex waited. "Oh, hell," he said. "I never filed the resignations. Technically you were both on personal leave."

Alex bit back a smile. "Thanks, Paul. I appreciate that."

"Yeah. Well, that Shofet woman suggested it. She seemed to think you'd be back. I suppose it's a bad idea for me to ask what you were doing."

"Very bad," Alex agreed.

"That's what I thought. I gotta tell you, though, I was expecting a funeral. Or two. I was kinda looking forward to wearing my new suit."

"Put it on," Alex suggested. "Take Jaguar out to dinner. Make sure she orders the lobster."

He flipped the receiver off and turned back to Jaguar.

"We're employed," he said.

"Of course," Jaguar said. "Paul may be a bureaucrat, but he knows good workers when he sees them."

* * * *

One Bird let Maya say goodbye to them after breakfast, just outside their house. She turned to Alex, held her arms out for an embrace he gave gladly. When she released him she turned to Jaguar and tentatively moved toward her. Jaguar pulled her in to hold her, and Maya buried her face in Jaguar's shoulder.

"You're still my mother," she said with the certainty of all truth.

"Yes," Jaguar agreed. "No matter what. And you know how to find me if you need me."

Maya pulled back, nodded solemnly, put her hand in One Bird's and skipped off to go herb gathering.

Jake stayed behind and walked with them to the airrunner. When they were there he rolled his gaze over the two of them, taking his time, making sure he saw everything he wanted to see.

"What you did," he said. "It was good. Didn't know if you'd come back, though."

"I was pretty sure we wouldn't," Jaguar said. "And you stalled me, didn't you? To let Alex get here."

"Didn't I say you weren't going alone?" Jake told her.

"Yeah. You did," Jaguar said. "But I don't know why you let Maya go, when it was so dangerous."

"She needed to make it right," Jake said. "She had a lot to make right. Besides, we told her to get back by suppertime, no matter what. *She* listened," he said, indicating that Jaguar never had. Probably never would.

"I wouldn't count on her always listening," Jaguar said. "She doesn't strike me as the type."

"I suppose. Alice and Red Feather'll have their work cut out for them. You'll come back sometimes to help. Both of you," he said, pointing at her and at Alex. "Come back and visit. Teach her a thing or two."

"We will," Alex promised. "With pleasure."

Jake peered up at the sky. "It's gonna seem small up there, after being out here with the big sky and the mother stones."

Jaguar nodded. "The land is smaller, but the space around it—that's as big as a dream, Jake."

* * * *

When the shuttle was on its way back, after they'd been given their drinks, Alex turned to Jaguar.

"Listen," he said. "We can't do this again."

"Hecate," she said. "I hope not."

"I mean hide the truth from each other."

She shifted in her seat, sipped at her drink. "I didn't lie to you."

"You didn't tell me who Senci was. You didn't give me enough information to make an honest choice."

"No," she admitted. "And you didn't tell me you put water in my hypos. If you told me, or I told you, we might both be dead."

"I'm not questioning what we did. I'm just saying that's over now. It has to be different. No more evasions."

She twisted around to look at him. "Not even from the Board? You think we should send them memos? Supervisor Alex Dzarny and Dr. Jaguar Addams would like to announce that they're fucking like bunnies. Well," she added thoughtfully, "Not bunnies, really . . . "

"I get the idea. But everyone suspected it long before it was true," he pointed out.

"The Board is okay with suspicion. It gives them something to talk about. But they don't appreciate visible truth."

He sighed. She was right. There were policies, protocols. If the Board knew, they might insist she change zones, or even Planetoids. But that wasn't the point right now. First, they had to settle themselves.

"That's the Board," he said. "What I'm talking about is between us. It has to be real. It's the only way this can work, and I'd like it to work. You understand that?"

She regarded him, her eyes quiet, more peaceful than he'd ever seen them. Something elemental had shifted in her. She took his hand and pressed it to her heart. Though they didn't need the physical contact to speak empathically, the gesture was a courtesy, an invitation. He touched the surface of her thoughts and found her open. Nothing hidden. At least, not from him.

All yours. No exceptions.

He felt the warmth of her thoughts, just on the edge of burning fire. Having made up her mind she would do this as she did everything else, at full throttle. He had a moment of disquiet, thinking he'd gotten more than he bargained for, then realized he wanted that, too.

She released him, curled her hand closed and ran her index finger down the side of his face. Then she leaned back in her seat and closed her eyes.

"When we get back—" he started to say, but had no idea how to finish the sentence. She helped him out.

"We'll be hungry," she said, eyes still closed. "Chinese?" she suggested. "My place?"

"That sounds fine," he said. "Just fine with me."

www.ingramcontent.com/pod-product-compliance
Lightning Source LLC
Chambersburg PA
CBHW050749250626
47155CB00005B/1986